NOWHERE
ON
EARTH

ALSO BY NICK LAKE

Satellite

In Darkness

Whisper to Me

NOWHERE

ON

EARTH

NICK LAKE

ALFRED A. KNOPF
NEW YORK

THIS IS A BORZOI BOOK PUBLISHED BY ALFRED A. KNOPF

Visit us on the Web! GetUnderlined.com

Educators and librarians, for a variety of teaching tools,
visit us at RHTeachersLibrarians.com

Library of Congress Cataloging-in-Publication Data is available upon request.
ISBN 978-1-9848-9644-5 (trade)
ISBN 978-1-9848-9645-2 (lib. bdg.)
ISBN 978-1-9848-9646-9 (ebook)

Printed in the United States of America
May 2020
10 9 8 7 6 5 4 3 2 1

First American Edition

For Leo, who was born alongside this story

CHAPTER 1

EMILY SAW THE mountainside only a moment before the small plane crashed into it. They were in thick fog; and then there was only whiteness, and noise, and pain. Before, Emily had always associated the color white with peace, with a kind of benign erasure. Snow smoothing out the angles of her lame little town. After that moment, she didn't.

She felt no fear. Her life did not flash in front of her eyes; she didn't see the things most important to her parade past, perhaps because they had already been taken away. No: her body was simply flooded with adrenaline: fight-or-flight response—though there was nothing for her to fight and nowhere to fly to, not anymore.

There was: the screaming of metal on metal, the shock that emptied her lungs, the white snow breaking in through the windows, the impact of her head on something, perhaps the side of the plane. It was a De Havilland Otter fitted with floats. This, thought Emily, was the kind of useless information she would take to the grave. Not that she would necessarily have a grave.

Even with modern technology, it was possible they would never be found.

And then: the realization.

Aidan.

She panicked, flailed, tried to catch his hand—the little boy, her brother. But her fingers closed on nothing.

Then, after the whiteness, the blackness.

CHAPTER 2

EMILY BLINKED BACK into light.

Part of a tree was sticking through the broken window; a cedar, she noticed uselessly. Her head was throbbing. She brought a hand up to it. Her temple and cheek were sticky with blood.

"Emily!" said a voice. The voice of a young boy, from behind her, oddly muffled. "Emily!"

Aidan.

Instinctively, she rose to stand and was roughly pulled back. She wrestled with the buckle on her seat belt, but it was bent and twisted away from her in the strange, unrecognizable new contours of the plane.

She looked around. There: on the seat next to her were shards of glass from the broken window. She picked one up and used it to saw at her belt.

"Emily!"

She cursed the restraint. The glass cut her—not badly, but slippery blood loosened her grip on it. "Coming. Coming," she said. Then the belt frayed and came apart. She lowered herself to the floor—nothing in her body seemed broken, but she couldn't be sure—and crawled into the aisle. Aidan. Aidan was the priority.

That was when she saw: the back of the plane was gone. There was only a vast round hole, the tears in the fabric of the aircraft revealing—in a way that was somehow disturbing over and above the fact of the crash—the insulation material inside the layers of metal. It opened a hole in her heart too. Wind whistled through. The rearmost row of seats was nowhere to be seen. The incline of the aisle continued uninterrupted into the downslope of the mountain, all low pines pooled with snow and deepening shadow.

It was still daylight, just, but up here, this far north and at this time of year, the night always folded itself into the day, swirled together with it. Time was a murky concept, the day an endless dusk, so it was hard to tell what time it was.

In reality, only a moment had passed since the plane had crashed—she thought. She had a concussion—she thought. She struggled to her feet and inched down the aisle. She noticed that she couldn't really hear her own movements. She looked into the row of seats behind her, where her *little brother* had been.

Nothing.

She swallowed a gasp, inaudible to her, like most everything else, her head jerking, casting her eyes around. But she'd heard him. She'd heard him, hadn't she?

"Emily!"

The muffled voice again.

He was at the back, near the snow, a little dark bundle in his black puffy jacket. She hadn't buckled him in. She'd done her own belt automatically but not his. Stupid. Selfish. She half walked, half slid down to him, past random boxes and packages. The plane was mostly a kind of unofficial mail service.

The soft confusion of hood and collar resolved itself as he turned and looked up at her. His eyes were huge, his skin pale. Looking to her for reassurance.

"It doesn't hurt," Aidan said. "But I'm stuck."

Emily kneeled. The floor of the plane had cracked, and like two tectonic plates sliding against each other, one part had pushed and jutted up over the other. Aidan's leg was caught in the gap between the old floor and its new, violent configuration.

Emily had seen a YouTube video once of a woman lifting a car off a toddler—but when she took the slanted floor and tried to raise it higher, it didn't move at all. Aidan didn't scream, but he sort of whimpered. Muscles she didn't know she had—and she knew her muscles well—tightened around her heart.

"It's OK," she said. "It's going to be OK." Her voice was damped, as if wrapped in snow. Flakes of it were whirling in through the hole where the plane's tail had been.

She saw a protruding metal bar, part of what had been the frame of a pair of seats. She pried it away from the rest of the structure, one end of it flattened, but still hard, still long.

"I'm going to lever the floor up," she said.

Aidan nodded. His pupils were large; frightened; animal. But at least they were both the same size. In Emily's ballet class back in Minnesota, a girl had fallen during a lift and hit her head, knocking herself out. Matching pupils were the first thing the paramedics had checked for.

She wedged one end of the bar into the gap, pushed it down

as hard as she could, and was more shocked than she should have been when it met with a hard, jarring resistance she recognized as belonging to half-frozen earth. The ground under the plane. Then she leaned all her weight on the other end of the bar, and with a creak she felt more than heard, the raised section of floor lifted.

Aidan scooted out, and as soon as he was clear, she dropped the bar and pulled him close. "Your leg?"

He touched it experimentally. "Fine, I think. There's a ringing in my head. Like a bell that won't stop."

"Yes," said Emily. "Mine too."

She pulled him to the side of the plane so they were sitting against the curve of it. He was light, small, easily movable.

"Will the plane explode?" he asked. His head came up only to her shoulder.

"I don't know," she said.

"I've seen that happen in movies," he said.

"Yes."

"From the fuel."

"Yes." She paused. "But it's snowing out there and, like, minus ten. In here we're sheltered at least. A little."

He looked skeptically at the snow dusting their clothes. "A very little."

A part of Emily's mind marveled at itself—calmly weighing the risk of being blown up against the risk of hypothermia. If only Miss Brady could see her now. Thinking of Miss Brady made her think of that last day at school: the orange and blue flames licking up the locker-room walls; the sirens; the sparks snowing, glowing red, into the sky.

She shook her head, refusing the memory.

She tried to think, to crystallize the options. Absurdly, her first instinct was to call Jeremy, ask him for advice, but he was a lifetime away in Minnesota, and anyway she'd left her phone at home—she hadn't wanted anyone to trace it.

She looked forward, toward the cockpit.

"I need to check on the pilot," she said.

Aidan turned his head. The back of the plane was a raw circle, a horrific *O*, with snow outside it. The front was a twisted mess leading to darkness. A scene from a wrecking yard.

"Um . . . ," he said.

He looked . . . scared. Worried. She hadn't seen it before, that expression on him, and it hurt her more than the cut on her head.

"Yeah" was all Emily could manage. She pushed herself up. "Wait here."

CHAPTER 3

USING WHAT REMAINED of the seats for support, Emily made her way slowly to the front of the plane. There was a partition between the pilot and the passengers—it was how she and Aidan were here in the first place. The door was shut, but that was a nominal state—it had bowed outward, the ceiling crushing down, and Emily could see clean through to the cockpit.

She held the handle and pulled—then braced herself and pulled even harder. The door screeched open wide enough for her to squeeze by. She'd always been small and flexible—that was how she'd ended up as the flyer on the cheerleading team. But she took up more room in the world than her size suggested. That was what her dad said. It wasn't a compliment.

She got through and found Bob Simpson, the pilot, splayed over the controls. She didn't know him, only his name. Spend a year in a small town in Alaska and you know most everyone's name. *He's dead,* she thought. She touched him. He wasn't dead.

Bob Simpson gave a low sigh and shuddered. Emily had no

clue what to do. Weren't you supposed to leave people where they were if they had a head injury? The way he was passed out over the instruments, he must have hit his head pretty hard. When Jade Allbright had fallen out of that lift and onto the studio floor, the instructor had put her in the recovery position, curled up there, like a question mark.

On the other hand, if Emily left him here and the plane *did* explode . . . As one part of her brain tried to work out whether she could and should move him, another part screamed at her to get out of the plane before it blew up, before it burst into flames. She ignored that part.

She couldn't tell if Bob was OK. But she did see his SPOT device—his emergency GPS beacon. They made them small enough that you could clip them on a cap—which was what her dad did. This one had fallen from the dash of the cockpit—did you say *dash?*—onto the floor of the plane, and was now right at her feet.

She turned back to the pilot. Move him? Or not?

Then he sat up, undoing the dilemma.

Half his face was sheeted with blood. When he saw her, he frowned. "Are you . . . an angel?"

She raised an eyebrow at him.

"Right, clearly not. . . . Forget it. It's pretty obvious I'm not dead because my head hurts like someone hit me with a tire iron." He looked at the broken window, the snow beyond. "I crashed," he said.

"Give the man a prize," said Emily.

"But what are you . . . *Who* are you . . . ?"

"Emily," she said.

He looked more closely at her, his expression shifting to a different quality of frown. "The Perez kid?"

"Uh-huh."

"Aren't you the one who—"

"Yeah."

He nodded slowly. Almost respect in it. Recognition. They were rebels, these Alaska bush pilots. Renegades. "And Miss Brady? It's still her, right?"

It was still her. It would always be her. Hair pulled so tight in a bun it looked like she was smiling. She wasn't when Emily was around.

"Suspended me."

"Figures." He felt in his denim-shirt pocket and took out a squashed pack of cigarettes. American Spirit. Only a bush pilot would smoke no-filters. Only a bush pilot would light one when he'd just crashed a plane into a mountainside. He flicked it out and into his mouth, and produced a lighter from another pocket. "I'm Bob. Bob Simpson," he said.

Emily nodded. "I know."

Bob lit the cigarette. Emily winced. Was he not aware that there could be leaking fuel pretty much anywhere?

"But listen, Emily Perez, of small-town notoriety," he said. "What are you doing on my plane? You're not on my manifest."

Emily wasn't totally sure what *manifest* meant, but she understood the point. "I stowed away," she said.

"You . . . stowed away? What is this, an adventure story?" He blew out smoke; it stung her eyes.

"It is, since you crashed the plane." Outside it was cold, and dark, and they were in the middle of nowhere. This wasn't good for Aidan. Not good at all.

He grimaced. "Not my fault."

"Not your *fault*? You're the pilot."

"I log five thousand miles a year, kid. Something went . . . wrong. The fuel-supply line, I think. I radioed, but it was too late."

"You radioed?"

"Yep."

Damn.

Emily looked out the window, as if there was anything to see. It was only white out there. One side of the cockpit was ripped open, rock and ice breaking through. "We should get out of the plane," she said. "Can you move?"

"I think so. Shoulder's dislocated, I reckon. And I knocked myself out pretty good. But I don't feel anything else."

He eased himself out of the seat, screaming only once, when he had to twist his back, which Emily thought was quite impressive. He scanned the controls in front of him, then looked at the damaged side of the cockpit. "You see a little orange thing with buttons on it?" he said.

"Like a SPOT tracker?"

He looked at her, surprised.

"My dad hunts," she said.

"Right. Yeah, exactly like that."

A moment. "No. But come on. My little brother is back there."

He cursed. "That tracker could be anywhere. We'll have to hope they got a fix on my signal when I made that distress call. Now . . . Wait—your little *brother*?"

"He's too small to look after himself. We've got to keep him safe." The plane. Leaving. It had all been for Aidan. And now that they'd crashed . . . it was still true, just in a different way. If she could keep Aidan safe . . . it would mean she'd have done something. Something big. With her life.

She'd have saved his.

Now, of course, with the plane smashed into the side of a mountain, it was going to be an awful lot harder. She shivered, thinking of the white vastness out there, trackless and blank.

"OK," said Bob, breaking her train of thought. "But if you and your kid brother die, it's not on me. You're not on my manifest."

She nodded. That was fair. But they weren't going to die. Definitely not Aidan. Not if she had anything to do with it.

Her fingers brushed against the pocket of her jeans, the small bulge there, where she had put the SPOT tracker. She felt it must be pulsing at Bob, beaming out its location—a heat, almost, came from it, burning her leg—but of course he didn't notice at all.

CHAPTER 4

IT WAS DARK now. Or at least the sun had set. There was a lot of light from the stars and moon.

Emily had wrapped Aidan in two blankets, for shock and because he was easily chilled at the best of times. They were sitting at the new, torn entrance to the plane. She was wearing her hooded fleece-lined winter jacket, which she'd stowed under her seat before takeoff.

Bob braced himself against the wing that was still attached to the plane, pushed his shoulder into it, and twisted. Emily realized he was trying to pop his dislocated joint back into place. He did it again—and screamed. He staggered for a moment, as if he might pass out, but steadied himself.

He moved his arm tentatively. Then he nodded and grunted. Started gathering supplies. He set down a gas can next to various objects he had already taken from the plane: a rifle, a rope, a sheet of thin metal. Behind them, the peak of the mountain loomed, a blacker mass in the dark of the night. Below, the foothills stretched toward a glow on the horizon. A town? The ocean? Emily wasn't sure.

"We've got food," the pilot said. "Plus the usual stuff I keep in case of emergency. Had a crate of water too, but it's somewhere down the mountain. Still, if we get a fire going, we can melt snow—should be able to camp here until someone finds us. We'll build the fire by the plane, use gasoline to get it going." He indicated the ground in front of him.

"*Here?* What if it . . . sets fire to the fuel tank?"

"Fuel tanks," he said. "Plural. And they're above the landing gear." He slapped the side of the plane. "This part of the fuselage is just metal bulkhead. It's our best bet in terms of shelter."

Emily looked at the plane. Or rather, the pieces of it. A plane was something that flew, something with wings. This was just a jumble of broken things. Bob was right, though: around them were only conifers, buried in snow. They offered some shelter, but not as much as the body of the plane.

She took in the gas tank, the snow, the ceiling of the plane and the space inside for protection from the elements.

Her dad always said: water, shelter, fire. Find those things quickly, in that order of priority, or you die.

Once, they'd been caught by a storm in the Adirondacks, too many miles out from the cabin they were supposed to be staying in that night. It had still been full daylight, but within an hour her father had found a stream, made a bivouac, lit a fire. *We get cold and dehydrated,* he said, *and we die.* And that hadn't even been in Alaska. Emily wanted to move, to keep moving, but reluctantly admitted the best course of action was to shelter here. "You're right," she said.

"Let's build that fire," said Bob.

Aidan looked up. "Do you have marshmallows for roasting?"

Emily raised an eyebrow at him.

Bob grunted, a half laugh. "If you find any, knock yourself out."

He sent Emily into the trees to find fallen branches to burn. She set off through the snow—grateful for the leather boots she was wearing but surprised by how tiring it was to walk in the deep powder. She gathered a few branches and dragged them back, sweating, even though the air was freezing in her nostrils. Then they broke open some of the packages from the plane and tore up the cardboard—it was drier and thinner than the wood.

With Emily's dad, it was all military precision and attention: tinder, kindling, firewood. Bob had a different approach. He just made a pile of cardboard and wood, doused it with gasoline, and set fire to it.

The rush of heat was immediate: something primitive, almost alive. The flames shot up, casting a glow on the side of the plane, made the nearby trees flicker and their shadows grow and recede, like breath. The mountain disappeared, and the horizon: they were in a glowing bubble now, surrounded by blackness.

Aidan glanced around. "Quite visible," he said, "these pyrotechnics."

It was exactly what Emily had been thinking. She squeezed his hand, as if to say, what could they do?

Then she saw that Bob was staring at Aidan, brow creased.

"Aidan's . . . um . . . different," she said. "Special."

Bob nodded slowly.

"We should eat," she said, so he would stop looking at her little brother.

They opened cans at random: corn, tuna, beans. Even Coke, to drink. There were also cookies and chips, but Bob said to save some stuff for later. He pulled one of the broken seats from the plane and set it up next to the fire. Then he yanked a first-aid kit from under it and took out a bandages, alcohol, cotton balls, scissors.

He walked over to Emily, snagging a water bottle from his pile of stuff, and motioned for her to look up at him.

"This will hurt," he said, pointing at the cut on her forehead.

"I know," said Emily.

This will hurt: it was practically her motto, she'd heard it all her life. Those years of pointe shoes, building up the strength in her toes, losing nails, developing calluses as hard as horn. Hiking with her dad. Even Miss Latimer ("call me Rachel"), the cheerleading coach from this past year in Alaska, had said it, about learning the routines. But it wasn't the routines that Emily had found painful. Not that.

Bob poured water over her forehead—some of it ran into her nose and mouth, and she coughed; turned involuntarily—and when she faced the right way again, he rinsed off the blood before using the alcohol and a cotton ball to clean the wound at her hairline. Finally he put a bandage on it.

"I'm no medic," he said. "But that will at least improve your odds."

Emily and Aidan sat on the lip of the fuselage, and Emily shuffled up close to the little boy, wrapped her arm around him, held him close. For warmth.

"Will someone find us?" Aidan asked.

"I don't know," she said. She squeezed him tight. "I don't know."

She was watching the fire: the shifting colors of it; the constant ribboning movement. Vertical liquid, leaping up from the branches but of them too, using them up—their hot ghosts escaping into the air. There was something unnatural and natural about it at the same time. The way the locker room had gone up, back at her school: as if it had wanted to be turned to black powder, had just been waiting for the fire to start, so it could return to its purest state.

She kept watching the flames. Burning through the wood, turning it to ash, doing what it wanted, what it was made for.

She envied it.

She hadn't danced a single time since they'd moved. Like a protest, only she didn't know whose benefit it was meant to be for. It wasn't like her mom noticed.

The fire mesmerized her. Always Emily kept half an eye on Bob, though. He seemed harmless enough—had barely glanced at her, his face impassive. But she was wary. He was a man, after all. And not seeing anything didn't guarantee safety. There were blank white landscapes, sometimes, in which wolves invisibly moved.

When the fire had burned down a little, Bob took the thin sheet of metal he'd found, and bent it into a rough semblance of a pan. Then he piled snow on it and pushed it—with a branch—into the embers at the side of the fire. The snow melted quickly, and he hooked out the rough cookware and poured the water into empty cans for them to drink.

Emily handed one to Aidan first.

"Where are we?" she asked, when they were done drinking.

The pilot glanced at the mountains all around them. They were near the top of one; some kind of glacier above them, and below them a sloping expanse of forest. "Somewhere in the Wrangell–St. Elias National Park," he said. "I was heading to Anchorage."

"I know," said Emily.

He narrowed his eyes. "You wanted to get to Anchorage?"

"Sure."

"Running away from home?"

"Something like that," she said.

"Because of the school thing?"

"Sure," she said again. It wasn't that. But how could she explain about Aidan? Though, she had to admit, even if she hadn't had to leave, she'd have wanted to. Not that she could explain that, either. How the town was like *Gilmore Girls* without the jokes. Like *Lost* without the mystery. No Jeremy to talk to, except on WhatsApp. The school was tiny compared to her last. And she had to do cheerleading instead of ballet.

Cheerleading.

Brad.

She closed her eyes and saw flames licking up the locker-room wall, heard the cheers, the noise of the crowd, the wolf whistles; felt Brad's hand on her ass and—

"You OK, kid?" said Bob, standing over her.

She opened her eyes, blinked. "I'm fine."

He raised his eyebrows. "Seems that fire's got you in a trance."

"I'm fine," she said again. She shifted farther into the plane, away from the fire. Aidan shuffled back with her, and she pulled him in close, trying to share her warmth with him.

Bob went and fetched more blankets for them. He watched as Emily silently wrapped one around Aidan. "Quiet, isn't he?" he said to Emily.

Emily nodded.

"I want Mom and Dad," said Aidan, looking up at him. "I want Goober. I can't sleep without him."

"Goober?" said Bob.

Emily looked at Aidan for a long beat, then back at the pilot. "His stuffed monkey. He fell out of the plane, I think."

"Goober keeps the monsters away," said Aidan.

"Is that right?" said Bob, but his face had relaxed a bit. Like this was more the kind of kid talk he expected. "He's a tough monkey, huh?"

His tone was friendly but a little stiff—like someone who has nieces or nephews but doesn't see them that much, Emily thought.

"No," said Aidan. "But he's always burping, and the monsters think it smells gross."

"Oh." A blink. "OK."

"Don't worry, though," said Aidan. "If they come in the night, I'll burp at them too." He patted his tummy. "We had Coke."

"Uh-huh, we did," said Bob. He smiled at Emily. "Let's get some sleep."

Later, when the pilot was snoring, deep in the cabin by the cockpit, Emily snuggled close to Aidan.

"What was that about Goober?" she said.

"Improvisation," he said.

"Well . . . OK. But, like, try to warn me next time."

"How far is it from here to Anchorage?" he asked.

"Far. Hundreds of miles, probably. And I'm not even sure which way."

Silence.

"We can't walk it?"

"No," she said.

Silence again.

"So we're lost?"

"Not yet," she said. "Not yet. I'm going to get you home, I promise."

CHAPTER 5

WHEN EMILY WOKE, the fire had gone out. She breathed in freezing air; breathed it out as mist. The cold was absolute: like all of winter in one day. It hurt her throat and chest; it put blades in the atmosphere.

She wrapped her blanket around Aidan, who was still sleeping, or seeming to. She got up and pulled on her boots.

"Where are you going?"

Small, sleepy voice. Aidan.

"To fetch wood. Stay here, I won't be long."

"Can I come?" he said.

"Won't you get cold?"

"Not if I'm moving."

Emily smiled and nodded. She liked having him by her side. She always had. She couldn't explain it: she'd just loved him, right from the start, the same way she'd loved ballet, from the moment she learned the first positions; he was like dance to her, like freedom. And now that dance was gone, there was only him. His hand fitted into hers like a key into a lock.

Always, and now, he held her hand and they walked together. They headed to the tree line.

"We can't stay here," said Aidan. "We need to keep moving. To Anchorage."

"I know," said Emily. "But we need fire first. And then . . . we'll plan."

"What will we tell Bob?" he asked.

"I have literally no idea."

Quickly, before her hands seized up, she gathered some twigs and fallen branches. *Gloves,* she thought. *Need to find some gloves.*

Aidan put out his arms, a request, and she placed a few small branches in them. Not too many.

"That OK?" she asked.

He nodded. He was smart, but he was so small, so fragile. She followed, her heart contracting at the sight of his tiny figure, holding the branches—so big in his small arms.

They walked back to the plane. Past the wing that had broken off and was lying in the snow. Bob had clearly woken with the same idea as Emily: he was dragging a branch, covered in needles, to the fire. It wouldn't burn easily; her dad would have sneered. But she supposed Bob was counting on the gasoline as an accelerant. Her dad would have sneered at that too, but she had to admit it was effective.

She wondered how old the pilot was. He had gray at his temples, but she wasn't good at guessing the age of adults. Forty? Fifty? It was hard to tell. He didn't seem older than her dad, but he didn't seem younger, either. Different, though. Her dad was all ex-military square lines: shaved, boxlike. Everything in its compartment. Tools: he hung them on racks in the shed out back, neatly. Sometimes she thought the main reason he didn't like his knee injury, apart from how he'd blown his military career along with his cruciate ligament, was that it offended his sense of neatness to have one leg that worked better than the other.

Bob, on the other hand, seemed more like a ... The word that came to her mind was *buccaneer.* Blurred at the edges.

Before Emily left Minnesota, Jeremy had told her that Alaskan pilots were "cowboys of the cold"—Jeremy often said things like that, a little overblown. He was fascinated by the bush pilots: their exploits, their bravery, their stubbled chins and hard arms too, their eyes washed pale by vast skies. She had teased him about it.

Her mom didn't like them so much. After their flight into Stafford Landing, a year before, she'd vowed that they'd never go on one of the little planes again. The pilot hadn't been Bob, but his vibe had been similar: unkempt, a loose cannon. Her mom had said, "If I'm going to trust my life to someone, I want it to be someone who can press a uniform."

Or, Emily thought, glancing at Bob in his jeans and puffy jacket, *wear* one.

Emily's mom worked part-time and had spent a lot of time in the gym when they lived in Minnesota; even now she still went running every day. She loved motivational quotes and inspirational poetry and the idea of personal growth through hard work and dedication—she was big on the power of transformation.

When Emily had joined the cheerleading squad at her new school, her mom had been thrilled. Which made one of them. Her mom had never really understood dance—she made that clear. She didn't understand what it was *for.* As if everything had to be for something, as if everything needed to be cheered and paraded. All those motivational magnets . . . and not a single work of art in the house, apart from a Jack Vettriano print that some aunt had given her as a housewarming gift. Jeremy had said, "Your mom is the kind of person who finds Instagram poetry inspiring."

Cheerleading, she totally got: it was supporting the football team. It was squad goals or whatever. It was motivational, like her magnets.

Emily thought squad goals could go screw themselves.

Anyway. Alaska was, like, the last frontier of flying—on that Mom and Jeremy would agree, though they'd disagree on the romance of it. A place where a person could test themself. A place you could still get lost, if you wanted to—or did if you weren't careful.

Emily thought about that, looking at Bob. He was the kind of person who might have wanted to get himself lost. Well: he was truly lost now. She winced at that thought.

"You ever crashed before?" she asked.

The pilot looked up. "Nope."

"Ever been lost in the wilderness before?"

"Nope."

She nodded. "That's comforting."

"They'll come," he said. He didn't sound too convinced. Alaska was a big place. "They'll see the smoke, don't worry."

She squinted up. The mountain was wreathed in fog. "Hmm," she said.

But that was exactly what she was worrying about—that they might come. Some people wanted to be lost, and she was one of them.

"Is there anything to eat?" asked Aidan, standing at the entrance to the plane. He was wearing a blanket like a shawl. He got cold very easily.

There was a *whoosh* as Bob doused the fire with gasoline. Flames rose into the air, standing on their own, glowing pondweeds, undulating, and Emily felt a surge inside her. The wood crackled. She noticed that her hearing was getting better; it had been muffled since the crash, sounds made fuzzy and faraway. From the woods came creaking noises—the trees buckling under their coats of snow. She beckoned Aidan closer to the heat: she didn't want him collapsing on her. That could raise a lot of questions.

"Here," said Bob. He threw a package of bread to Aidan, who fumbled it and dropped it. He bent and picked it up.

"Might as well eat it now," said the pilot.

Aidan ate a slice of bread; handed one to Emily. She smiled at him, and he smiled back, a real smile. He was learning to do that.

Despite herself, she edged a little closer to the fire and held out her hands to warm them, staring into the wild, fickle flames. Because she of all people knew that fire had two faces: the one that said home, and the one that burned things down.

She thought of that fire, part of the reason she was here on this mountainside. How her mom had stopped jogging, because people on the street would stare at her. How her dad came home early from school every day, because, he said, he couldn't go into the staff room anymore.

She hadn't meant it to happen. She didn't *like* fire: though, when it had happened, she found she liked the way it took ordinary things—clothes, wood, a whole building—and made them flare, made them glow, made them beautiful; and then made them nothing but ashes. It had been . . . cathartic.

Anyway, she didn't care what people thought of her. She hated them all. Small-town kids. With their friends, knowing only each other, knowing what they wanted. Or just wanting what they were given.

Never wanting more. Never wanting to get out.

She looked around, at the wilderness. *Although,* she thought. *Be careful what you wish for.*

Now she was stuck on a mountainside in the Alaskan spring, which was not as full of warmth and new growth as that season suggests elsewhere. It was barely above zero, even with the sun up.

"What's that?" said Aidan, and she put away her memories, *swish,* like minimizing a window on an app, and turned back to him, the little boy maximized. Bright. Backlit.

"What?"

He was pointing downhill. There was a kind of rumbling sound coming from that direction, something rhythmical, deep and beating.

"That," he said. He looked scared.

CHAPTER 6

BOB FROWNED AT the noise. Emily's eyes flicked to the rifle leaning against the side of the plane. Deer. She knew how to shoot. Had done it a lot with her dad, her mom too. Dressed in bright orange, so other hunters would see them. During the season. All day out in the woods; the whole thing. Her parents' dream—her nightmare.

Her eyes still on the rifle, she took Aidan's hand and held it. She could feel his heartbeat through his fingers. *Da-dum. Da-dum.* It felt so real; the only thing that was real.

Then from the treetops below them rose dark spinning movement, wide and flat. Rotor blades.

The body of the squat black helicopter followed its blades into the murky sky; heavy and unlikely seeming. Its nose angled downward, and it roared forward, then lowered itself toward the slope of snow in front of them, on the clearest patch, where the rocks and trees were thinnest.

Emily's eyes were scopes, her mind a calculator. *A hundred yards,* she thought. *Hundred and twenty, maybe. Wind strong.*

From the—she thought back to the sun and where it had risen, the wind blowing from the opposite direction—*the west.*

It was stupid, she realized afterward. It was stupid, but she just expected, somehow, that Bob would know. That he would do the same as her. She pulled Aidan back, started to fade into the plane. To disappear. She knew how to do that; it was how she'd survived at school. Until Brad saw her. Until they suspended her.

Men in white snowsuits jumped down from the helicopter. They began walking up the slope, slowly but with purpose in their movements. They were wearing black masks. To protect them from the snow whipped up by the rotors, maybe.

Or to stop people from seeing their faces.

Maybe.

But Bob didn't know anything, of course, so he didn't do what she did. He didn't fade into the background.

He stood tall, arms up, and waved his hands in and out, almost crossing, the wave of every person wanting to be rescued. One of his arms didn't quite reach the other, dangled awkwardly when he lowered it: the lingering pain of his dislocation.

"No—" Emily started to say.

But there was no time.

One of the white-clad men raised something, a long black stick that had been down by his side, blending in with the shadows of the low sun, the always presence of night, here in Alaska, in the corners of things.

He put the stick to his shoulder in one smooth movement and fired, and Bob fell backward, blood spraying in what, Emily thought in the strange clarity of that frozen moment, seemed awfully like the explosion of a red firework against the white background. But she didn't have time to worry about Bob.

She dived into the snow, pulling Aidan behind her like a small dragged mannequin, then yanked him to his feet and ran, half carrying him, away from the fire, into the shadows. Where they would be harder targets.

CHAPTER 7

EMILY, STILL TOWING Aidan, hunkered down behind the broken-off wing of the plane. She peered over it, down the mountainside. The men in white suits were moving steadily up, sweeping with their guns, taking no chances. She counted them: one, two, three, four.

Four men.

And on their side: her, a wounded or possibly even dead pilot, and a seven-year-old boy. Apparently.

Not good odds.

She held Aidan's hand, got ready to run, to scramble, up the mountain and through the trees.

Closer by, between her and the soldiers—or whatever they were—she saw Bob struggle to a sitting position, hand clamped over the top of his arm where, she guessed, he'd been hit.

Shit, she thought. *Shit, shit.* She couldn't leave him here. But he was going to slow them down.

Her eyes flicked again to the men with the guns.

"Can you . . . ?" she said to Aidan.

He shook his head. "Too far away. I can't do anything."

"OK. OK." Her mind seemed to want to repeat things, to stutter. Like it was trying to go back in time to before any of this was happening. Going back in time was what she'd wanted for ages, of course. To Minnesota, to dance exhibitions, to Jeremy. Although now that would mean losing Aidan, and she wouldn't do that, couldn't do that. With Aidan, it was like her heart had been taken out of her and given a body, so it could move around the world on its own.

"Wait here," she said to Aidan.

Then she came out from behind the wing at a running crawl, moving down toward Bob. She got one arm under his good one, and—while hissing at him, "Don't say anything, just move"—she hauled him and he hauled himself back up and away from the men with guns. A percussive bang echoed off the mountains, and a bullet zipped over their heads. Then another kicked up snow by her foot. The figures in white were moving.

"Move," she said again. Freeze-frame. Rewind. Stutter, stutter.

In the glow of the fire she saw the rifle from the plane casting a long, thin black shadow onto the fuselage. She gave the pilot a push in the back, to safety behind the wing, and jagged left as a bullet grazed her elbow—she felt nothing for a moment, and then hot sharp pain and a warm bloom as her sweater soaked with blood.

Ow.

But she was moving that arm, swinging it to grab the rifle, so she knew the wound wasn't serious. She held the gun by the stock and booked it toward the separated wing, boots slipping on the snow; dropped by the fire to rake her fingers through the ash at its edge—she didn't want a clean reflective scope lens giving away her exact position—wincing as it burned her skin; then on to the shelter of the wing. A bullet thudded into it as she flung herself down.

No time to think, no time to consider.

The gun was loaded. It was a Browning with a detachable box magazine. Her dad would have been contemptuous. *You're hunting deer,* he'd have said. *Not fighting a war. What do you need a magazine for?*

Well.

Emily took a deep breath; held it. She was counting on surprise. She kneeled, wiped the soot from her hand on the scope. She had to improvise. Her dad's hunting rifles all had modern multicoated antireflective scopes, but this was an old rifle—single-coated, if that. She had to cut down on the glare of the glass from the fire or it would give away her location.

Then she raised her head over the wing, swung the rifle up in a smooth, practiced movement, every reluctant hunting trip with her parents singing in her nerves, living in the memory of her muscles. Her dad liked her to practice things, like aiming a rifle, over and over again. Until the memory was deep inside her, had become physical. He'd kneel beside her, sweating from the pain in his knee: wanting her to be perfect, strong, the warrior he didn't get to be anymore. It was a pain. Literally. Her mom was the same, obsessed with strength. Emily guessed it was one of the things that had drawn them together.

Still, that discipline was coming in useful now.

Emily looked down the scope, found the first man, twenty yards away. He wasn't looking at her; the soot would keep any gleam from the flames off her scope, she hoped.

She didn't want to kill him. She aimed at his leg, his thigh, tracked it as he moved. She let out the breath she'd been holding but didn't breathe in again. Perfectly still. If she hit his femoral artery, he'd die, but his calf was too small a target.

Half squeeze on the trigger. Breath still held. She thought of something her dad had said: *It isn't until you're right there, in the theater of war, that you find out if you can do it.* Whether you could shoot a man; whether you had that coldness in the core of you. Whether all your training was for nothing.

This wasn't war, but it was close.

She felt no hesitation, just calm.

She centered the man's leg in the scope, dimmed by the ash but perfectly visible. She thought of Aidan, and getting him to Anchorage, and then to safety, forever. She thought of Pastor Norcross, quoting the Psalms. "Rescue the weak and needy; deliver them from the wicked."

She was rescuing Aidan, wasn't she?

Fire.

The gun was well looked after. It kicked, but the bullet flew true; the man went down with a shriek, the other three men swinging around to look at him instead of looking up toward Emily, which was a mistake.

Well, she thought. *It turns out I can do it.*

I'm cold.

I'm ice.

She just missed the second guy she took a shot at—he moved as she fired.

She allowed herself to pause, to think—but only for an instant. The other three men were running now, keeping low, moving up the hill toward her. Fast. She was impressed. Training over fear, after that initial confusion.

Through the scope, she could see a yellow tank attached to the struts of the helicopter, about the size of a big courier box. Preparation. A long search. Impossible to return to base and re-fuel. So they had brought fuel with them. It was a spare tank.

She let out another breath, held the scope steady, aimed at the yellow cube. And fired.

The explosion was a breath made manifest, the whole field of snow a lung: there was a *crump!* as it sucked in cold air, and then the shock of the exhale, the shivering *boom!* as the helicopter stopped being and became a ball of fire instead; a primary explosion and then an even bigger one, as the main fuel tank caught.

The rearmost of the three men in white was thrown to the ground, face-first; he didn't move at all. Dead, Emily guessed, but she wasn't sure. She felt a lurch in her stomach at the thought, like the world had come away from its hinges and was swinging wildly. The other two men turned in shock, guns waving uselessly at their sides.

Emily, ears ringing, ducked down next to Aidan and Bob.

"What the *hell*?" said Bob, face white and drained of blood, because of the pain, she imagined. "Who are they? Who turned you into Rambo Girl?"

"Later," said Emily.

"What?" said Bob. "We're getting shot at and you want to explain later?"

"Yes," she said. "Because we're being shot at."

His eyes closed for an instant; then he opened them again. "OK . . . so what *now*?"

"I have no idea," said Emily.

"But you . . . all of that . . . you just did . . ."

"I grabbed a gun. I didn't have a *plan*."

Aidan tapped her on the arm. "I do," he said.

CHAPTER 8

"YOU DO?" SAID Bob, turning. Skeptical but hopeful too, deep down. That was Emily's whole mode of being—the skeptical part anyway; it made her warm to him. She was working on the hopeful part, since Aidan. She still hoped, even now, that she could get him out of all this.

"The wing," said Aidan. "Use it as a sled. To go downhill." He was hugging the blanket around him, and Emily was horribly conscious that they were far from the warmth of the fire. She edged closer to him, pressed herself against him.

"That's . . . that's not bad," said Bob. "If we can get it moving."

Emily looked at him, then at the wing. It was big. Heavy. But the slope was steep—at least it was once you got past the fire. The wing was almost upright—they would have to push it over, so that its smoother side was against the snow. Damn it. Everything was going so fast, and it was the only plan they had. "I'll fire twice," she said. "Then we push."

"Wait," said Aidan.

"What?"

"I need something." He started to move back toward the plane, away from the shelter of the wing.

"No—" began Emily, but it was too late; he was running now, hunched over, head ducked down. Shots streaked above him, turning by mechanical magic into bullet holes, like silver flowers, in the blue body of the plane.

Aidan disappeared into the torn opening in the fuselage. Moments passed. Emily couldn't have said how long; the world was reduced to her breathing, in and out. She glanced once, over the wing, and saw that the two men still moving were only a dozen yards away, maybe a bit more. Then the small figure of her brother appeared at the gaping mouth of the plane, and began hurrying back to them.

"Thanks," he said, hitting the snowy ground beside them in a surprisingly impressive knee slide. He must have seen it in a film or something.

Emily popped up. The first guy was too close for her to use the scope; she just fired in his general direction, and he ducked. Turned, fired again at the other.

"Now!" she said.

She and Bob got their shoulders against the wing. Emily thought she heard the man sobbing—one arm dislocated and the other with a bullet in it—though her hearing was not good now, everything echoing and muffled, as if the snowy mountains were inside her, their blurred acoustics, damped by frozen water.

They heaved, feet slipping in the snow, the effort turning Emily's body into hard, taut sinew and muscle, something engineered. The wing tipped, then sloshed down onto the slush near the fire. They kept going—and it began to slip downhill.

"Go, go, go!" she said. She got an arm under Aidan, and Bob did too, and they slung him up and onto the top of the wing—he was exposed then, but there was nothing else they could do, and he clung tight to it, flattening himself as a bullet whined over his head. Then Emily threw herself up and forward, got her top half onto the wing, squirmed up until she was lying facedown next to Aidan, an arm around him to hold him tight. She glanced right and saw that Bob was on too, and they were accelerating, gathering speed down the slope.

They passed one of the men in white, and he spun, rifle pointing at them, fired an automatic burst that hammered against the wing. Emily clutched Aidan's hand, pulled herself even closer to him and him closer to her, so she was wrapped around him, almost, as they swished over the snow, going quickly now, toward the tree line.

She pressed him to her. For warmth. For protection.

Suddenly she realized: they would hit a tree and stop and that would be it.

But they didn't.

They shot smoothly through a stand of pines, and on the other side was a wide, long expanse of snow, almost like a ski run, all the way down to a forested hill above a river, far below. Faster and faster they went, snow whipping their faces, the cold air rushing, a thing of form, not emptiness, like water, flowing over them and into their eyes, the hiss of the wing as it glided downhill like anxiety and relief made into sound.

It was then that she realized their mistake: they had only the clothes they were wearing, no blankets, nothing to wrap themselves in. The cold air hummed against the wing, as if singing of how it was going to kill them.

She hung on: to the wing; to Aidan. And balanced, feeling every shift and slide of the wing. Holding on was something she was good at. Balanced she had been, once.

But she was working on it.

It felt like a mile, two miles, they must have gone, down that long slope of snow, until they hit a rock just before the forest and were slingshot—a moment of pure weightlessness, tumbling, Emily trying to enfold Aidan with her body, to encase him in her strength—and crashed into a snowbank. Where the impact made her let go.

Aidan Aidan Aidan.

She fumbled desperately for his limbs, for the outline of his body. He was wailing with pain . . . until she realized he was laughing.

"You OK?" she said.

"I think so." He smiled. "Let's do it again."

She rolled her eyes at him.

They sat up, looking back at the mountain they had come down. There was no way the remaining men could follow, not without being seen. And they knew Emily had a rifle. Or at least, they *thought* she did. She had dropped it somehow, in the chaos of the slide. *Stupid, stupid, stupid.*

How many? she wondered. She wasn't sure if the explosion had killed the one who had fallen. So at least two but possibly three. And they'd be coming, rifle or no rifle.

"Well, goddamn," said Bob. He was lying flat on his back but then levered himself up. His gun-shot arm hung at his side. Blood staining his sleeve. They were going to have to do something about that.

"Can you walk?" said Emily. "We need to keep moving." She was thinking of those men, clad in white, their eyes covered, ready to shoot. They'd be coming, and they'd be pissed.

"Sure," said Bob. "But give me five minutes, OK, boss?"

She blinked. Nodded.

He took his cigarettes from his pocket, and his lighter. Emily shook her head at him. It was possible the men would see the flame, from up on the mountain. If they thought Emily and the others had been wiped out, if they'd seen the wing suddenly stop, and flip, then they may as well keep thinking that.

Bob sighed.

"I'm glad you have the lighter, though," she said. "That was smart, to bring it." She knew he'd just had it in his pocket, it had been there by default, but, well, it didn't hurt to flatter people, especially ones you were stuck with in a survival situation.

He smiled very slightly.

Yep.

They sat there for a moment longer, looking up at the mountain in the pale sunlight. They could see the orangey red of the still-burning helicopter, its smoking ghost rising into the air.

"So, are you going to tell me who the hell those guys are?" asked Bob. "I mean, I've done some air defense work, contract stuff for the military bases up here. And these guys, whoever they are, they're serious."

"I guess you could call them the men in black," Emily said.

"They were wearing white."

She stood, and helped Aidan up. "Yeah, well," she said. "It's snowy."

CHAPTER 9

THEY LEFT THE wing where it was. Emily wanted to keep moving. Needed to keep moving. So that Aidan would be safe.

"They'll be coming," she said. "The ones who are still alive. At least two of them. Maybe the other one too, the one who was knocked down by the explosion. I don't know if he's . . . dead or not."

A pang as she said the word *dead*. Something like a stitch, but in her heart. She had shot deer before; rabbits. She had not wanted, ever, to shoot a person. Even her dad, macho man extraordinaire, wouldn't talk about the people he'd killed in Iraq.

"Why?" said Bob. "What do they want?"

"Who," said Emily.

"What?"

"Who—not what—is what they want. But I'll explain later."

"No," he said. "You'll explain now." His eyes were hard, and he wasn't smiling even a little bit.

Emily touched his hand; it was a manipulative move, a power move, the kind of thing call-me-Rachel, her cheerleading coach, would have done, but she didn't have time to take it slow. "Listen," she said. "I *will* tell you what's going on. I mean, where am I going to go?" She gestured at the emptiness all around them. "But first I need to make sure you don't die, and we need to put some distance between ourselves and those assault rifles while there's still light."

She looked down as she said it, and he followed her eyes and saw the blood on the snow, from his bullet wound.

He took a breath. He knew as well as she did that daytime was a fleeting thing up here. "OK."

She made him sit on the rock they had crashed into, and looked at his upper arm. There were two distinct blossoms of blood on his sweater, front and back; the bullet had gone right through. That was good. She thought so anyway—she wasn't exactly experienced with bullet wounds, not ones in people, but she figured there was less chance of infection with the bullet not still inside.

On the other hand, there was more chance for it to have hit stuff as it went through—but if it had nicked an artery, he'd already be dead, right?

She wished she had a knife—a knife was pretty much an essential for survival generally and would have been useful now *in particular*—but instead she tore off one of the sleeves from her long T-shirt, then put her sweater and jacket on again. She couldn't really afford the loss of layering, the loss of warmth, but she couldn't afford for Bob to bleed to death, either. She made him take off his sweater—she saw the tears standing in his eyes, magnifying them, when he eased it over the wound.

She bent down and scooped up some clean snow, pressed it

into the wound as hard as she could. She figured it would clean the hole and slow blood flow at the same time. Then she wrapped her shirtsleeve around it as tightly as she could, tucking it under itself.

"Best I can do," she said.

"Thank you," he said. The mountain was doing something to their speech. Grinding it down to essentials.

She looked across at Aidan, who was watching her intensely, and she took his hand. It was cold in hers—that was bad.

"Are you OK?" she said, looking down at him. He was as pale as the sliver of moon in the sky above them.

"I think so," he said. "I have very little frame of reference."

"That kid freaks me out," said Bob.

Emily smiled weakly, leaned down, and kissed Aidan on the top of his head. "Yeah, me too," she said.

"You're going to give me the whole story, yeah?" said Bob.

"When we stop to camp," said Emily. "Let's get as far as we can from the plane first."

"I'm going to hold you to that," said Bob. "Remember, I'm the one with the lighter." There was heat in his voice, as if smoke might come out with his words. His eyes were round stones, un-yielding.

Emily looked at Aidan. He shrugged.

"Yeah," she said. "I remember." She turned, trying to orient herself. Her head was still spinning from the crash, but she could see the track they'd scoured in the snowy slope. As their pursuers would too. "Northwest is that way, right?" She pointed.

"Right," said Bob.

"So let's go."

CHAPTER 10

THEY SET OFF through the trees. Movement would keep Aidan from getting too cold. They were lucky in one thing: he was still wearing his puffy coat, the one she'd bought for him at Mackay's general store, but she worried it wasn't enough.

The snow was deep, powdery—hard to walk through, her weight pressing down into it. Aidan was walking more easily: he was lighter.

"Where are we going?" her little brother asked.

"Where we were always going," she said. "The antennas."

"Walking?"

"We don't have much choice," she said.

A pause as they picked their way through roots and snow.

Aidan put his hand in his jacket pocket and took out a plush toy monkey. He held it close.

"*That's* why you went back to the plane?" she said.

He glanced at her—a quick glance, which ran off her and down, like water. "Yeah. I wanted Goober. I found him under our seats."

"*Seriously?*" she said.

"Oh, come on," interrupted Bob. "Don't be hard on the kid. He wanted his toy."

A complicated expression passed over Aidan's face. Emily felt the earthquake friction of different layers of reality rubbing together.

"He could have been killed," she said eventually.

"He's just a kid."

Emily didn't say anything, but she gave Aidan's hand a squeeze, just one, hard. He was quiet after that.

So: Aidan had his monkey. Which she had also bought for him at the general store, because without her he would have had no clothing and no toys. They had a lighter. Boots—and she was glad she'd had the presence of mind to dress them both in good, sturdy ones. She was acutely conscious of everything they did not have, however. They did not have:

Water.

Food.

Clothing, beyond what they were wearing. It was a good thing she'd had her jacket on when the helicopter arrived.

Rope.

A knife.

The rifle, even.

But she *did* have herself, her own experience. All those trips with her mom and dad. God, she'd hated them at the time. *Living the dream.* That was what they called it. Being in the outdoors. Good for the soul. As if suffering, as if being cold and sore and covered in blisters and bug bites was going to make you a better person. She would have been happy becoming a better person by staying in her contemporary dance class in the city and not moving to a place where people thought jumping up and down to rock covers in the Crescent Moon bar was dancing.

Still, it was all there, or some of it, anyway, what had been drummed into her about survival. Shelter, fire, water, food. None of which, at this point, she had.

But she had:

Aidan.

And she had:

Her own will, and her own will was a knife; it had cut her away from the isolated town that was her new and only world, had made this different reality. She would kill the world with her bare hands, if the world came for Aidan, with the strength of her will, which was a knife. She would cut the world into a million pieces.

She squeezed his hand again, this time without realizing.

He squeezed back.

"I love you," she said.

"I know," he said matter-of-factly.

She laughed. "Jerk," she said.

He frowned at her, and she marveled at the things he still didn't understand.

Then she heard a rustle from the undergrowth over to their left, and held up a hand to stop the others.

An impression of brown fur, and she breathed out, relaxed—it wasn't the men with the guns. But then the fur advanced, grew, and was a bear.

She froze, all the breath out of her lungs, the warmth of it fading as it mingled with the Alaskan air.

CHAPTER 11

THEY COMMUNICATED WITH their hands and heads. Emily pointed to the bear and then made a shushing, calming gesture, palms down. Like: keep very still. It hadn't seen them yet. The trees loomed over them, casting long thin shadows on the snow.

Bob nodded, with more than an inflection of: *Yes, of course, what am I, an idiot?*

The bear was not long awake, this early in spring, Emily thought. Big and brown. Hungry. It could tear off a limb from a person like a person would tear off a chicken wing.

She pulled Aidan down toward the ground, toward the snow, and Bob crouched too. Emily pressed a finger to her lips, as if they needed telling. Bob, anyway. You didn't go disturbing bears so soon after hibernation.

Her own breathing roared in her ears. The bear was maybe fifty yards away, head low.

They crouched, Emily holding Aidan's hand tight in hers. She licked a finger and held it up. The wind was blowing from the bear toward them: that was good.

And the bear kept its head low, snuffling along through the undergrowth. She remembered something from a trip with her parents: in the spring, bears mostly foraged for berries and roots, instead of hunting.

Mostly.

She began to relax a little, though there was an ache deep in her thighs from crouching, and she couldn't sit—the snow would get on her clothes, and her dad always said, "You get wet, you die."

It felt like forever, but might have been twenty minutes, when the bear, at last, lumbered heavily away from them and into the forest. They straightened a little, to ease their joints. Bob and Emily did anyway. Aidan was quite small.

Then, after another ten minutes or so, they began to slowly move in the direction they'd been heading: northwest. Emily glanced at the sky worriedly. The sun was very low now. It would be dark soon, and the temperature would drop below zero.

They descended through a valley, over a brow, and then into another, smaller, valley. Bob was walking slowly, she noticed. Limping, and inhaling sharply when his unsteady footing in the snow caused him to twist his shoulder and arm.

They walked.

And they walked.

What must have been an hour passed. It was freezing, and Aidan was shivering—she could see him trembling. They needed to stop soon, to shelter.

There was a lake far below, on the other side of an outcrop of rock. The low sun gleamed on it—it was still iced over in the middle, tinged blue, but the outer parts were reflecting light in the shifting way that suggested water. Ringed with a stony beach, it looked like, then a layer of pine, a belt of what might be cotton-wood, thickets of cranberry bushes, probably, though it was the wrong season for the berries . . . and rock, and grass, up to where they stood.

Twin lakes, actually, Emily realized: one higher, feeding the other via a small river that this far off registered as white, from the spray.

And at the upper lake, a cabin. A low structure, wooden, one story. No smoke coming from it, so unoccupied, it seemed. A hunter's cabin, maybe. About a few miles away. A few clicks, her dad would have called it.

"Cabin?" said Emily to Bob.

"Yeah, I see it."

Too far away, though. Too far to reach before nightfall. Night was something that really did fall, this far north. Something dangerous. Like a guillotine.

"Can't reach it before dark," she said.

"Nope."

Emily scanned the small valley, noticed the shadow of the cliff to their left. It was sheer, the rock, and trees grew close to it, aspens and cedars.

"There," she said. "We'll make a lean-to shelter against the cliff."

"Oh," said Bob. "You know how to do that too, do you?" His voice caught on a snag of pain somewhere inside him, softened his sarcasm.

"Yes," she said neutrally.

She led the way downhill and to the left. Southwest, she could see, from the setting sun. Off-track, for where she and Aidan were going, but they had to stay alive before they could think about their final destination.

She found low-hanging branches, thick with needles, which she was able to twist until they snapped away from their trunks. She made Bob sit against the rock of the cliff, Aidan too, while she did it—gathering as many thick branches as she could. There was no point in Bob bleeding out, and she sure as hell wasn't going to let Aidan freeze to death.

She was sweating, soaking her clothes with it, and she knew she'd pay for that when the sweat froze, but she was grateful—in the moment—for the warmth. Anyway, if you didn't get shelter, you might as well butcher your own carcass and give it to the nearest vulture.

She paused to take off her jacket, made Aidan put it on over his own. He tried to refuse, but she could see the skin going pale, almost blue, on his face. She hugged him, until his shivering stopped, then carried on working. She didn't like the color of his skin.

She leaned the branches against the cliff wall, longest first, and then made a sort of weave across that. She left an opening in the middle, a very basic chimney, for smoke. No point insulating your shelter and then dying in your sleep of smoke inhalation.

An image: their first camping trip after moving to Alaska. Her dad had made a shelter just like this. Her parents' joy at this vast open landscape, at being finally in the wilderness for good; her fury at being trapped, confined, in so much huge emptiness. And yet, it had all gone in, somehow, the stuff she had learned, and it was keeping her alive now.

Still, if her family had never moved here, she would never have needed to know, to be kept alive.

But she wouldn't have Aidan, either.

Her mind went in circles like that: a fish in a bowl.

Meanwhile, she needed to build the fire.

At least Bob had the lighter, so they could cheat there. But the ground, she thought, the ground was a killer. Too cold—it would leach the life right out of you. She couldn't do much, but she forced herself to go out again into the trees, breath ghosting in front of her, arms aching, and gather more branches, soft ones dense with needles, which she laid on the ground, to form a kind of mat to sleep on.

Then: More wood, this time dead branches, no leaves, the drier the better. She got some, and then she got more, and then she got more. They didn't want to run out in the night. It was spring, but the temperature would easily fall to twenty below when it was full black. In the sky, the moon floated above the treetops, ribboned by thin mist: it was like something done with Day-Glo paint, then smudged with a finger.

She dragged the wood back and stacked it at one end of the shelter, then went back a final time, looking for leaves and moss, anything to use as tinder. She formed it into a pile in the middle of the lean-to. "Come in," she said, to Bob and Aidan.

Aidan scooted in, and she made room for him, then held out her hand to Bob, who had entered the shelter from the other side.

"You're going to light a fire?" said Bob. He looked up the mountainside in the general direction of the crashed plane. "With those men out there?"

"They *might* see it and find us and shoot us," she said. "But if we don't have a fire, we *will* die."

"I vote for not dying, personally," said Aidan.

Bob snorted, almost involuntarily. He inclined his head slightly.

"Lighter," Emily said to Bob, still holding out her hand.

He hesitated. She could see the thoughts behind his eyes. It was his only leverage, after all.

She rolled her eyes.

He gave her the lighter.

"Cigarette," she said.

"Oh," he said. "Didn't realize you . . ."

But she didn't want to smoke it—actually, she kind of did, it had been a shitty day, but that wasn't the point of asking for it. She didn't want to use up lighter fluid, was all. She lit the cigarette he handed her and took a deep drag; blew the smoke up her makeshift chimney, where it mingled with the stars above.

Then she held the glowing red cherry of it to the moss and leaves, until they caught; she let Bob take a drag, then moved the cigarette to the moss again, and repeated until the tinder was crackling—and then she felt the familiar rush as flame leaped from the pile like a miracle. Like a magic trick, like a genie, like none of those things at all, like only itself, hungry for stuff to make into flame and smoke, and the bigger sticks and twigs started to burn too.

She had been thinking about drinking water. She'd seen a concave stone, and wondered about using it as a sort of bowl, putting it by the fire for snow to melt in it. But the stone would get hot, and each time they'd have to cool it before they could hold it and drink from it, and you needed six liters of snow for every liter of water.

The only solution—or the only solution she could think of at that moment—was her boots. They were good ones; leather, waterproof. Her dad was big on the importance of reliable footwear. She usually hated that.

Anyway. It was going to taste gross, and she'd have to dry the boots after, or get frostbite, but it was all she had.

She took the boots off, keeping her socked feet close to the fire. She had cleared the snow from the ground under the shelter, so she crawled to the edge and packed the white stuff into her boots and then set them down by the fire, almost *in* the fire, as close as she dared.

"You can't be ser—" began Bob.

"Yes, I am," she said.

He pulled a face, then nodded.

A bootful of snow equaled a toeful of water, as she'd expected, and by the time she'd done it again and again and Aidan had drunk—first, she made sure of it; water was as important to him as it was to anyone—and she and Bob, they were all heavy-lidded with sleep.

"No food tonight," she said. "We'll deal with that tomorrow." Even though she was hungry. Even though her stomach was a twisting beast within her.

"But first . . . ," said Bob slowly. "You were going to . . . tell me what those men wanted. What's . . . happening."

Shit.

She took a breath, psyching herself up. She glanced at Aidan, but his face was blank.

Oh, thanks for the help, she thought.

Then she turned back to Bob, and his eyelids were fluttering, and he keeled very softly to the side, leaning against Aidan, and was asleep.

The man's breath came gentle and slow.

Emily felt a loosening inside her. Ridiculous, really: she was still going to have to tell him tomorrow.

But, then, anything could happen between now and tomorrow. She watched him, and Aidan too, until Aidan's eyes closed also, and his breathing too went soft and easy.

She closed her own eyes, but the flames were still there. Flames against a wall of metal. Miss Brady dragging her by the arm, away from the building as it went up. The wail of a wail of a wail of a siren—that going-nowhere repetition of it; insistent. And another too, sirens weaving into each other, both fire trucks in the tiny town.

And new things: the burst of blood from Bob's arm, spritzed into the icy air by the bullet. The shriek of the man she'd shot in the leg.

She sighed, and stood—moving to the edge of the shelter, near the entrance.

She went through some simple stretches. Hamstring, calf, thighs. Lunges and reaches. She needed more room to move. She stood in the opening, looked out. A light snow was falling. She imagined herself in the clearing just outside, turning in the snow, dancing. Warming herself up. But her boots were still drying by the fire, and anyway, she hadn't danced in a year.

When she turned back, she saw Aidan sitting up, looking at her expectantly.

"Go on," he said.

"No."

"For me. I've never seen you do it."

She looked down at him, sighed, put on a serious face, and did a perfect arabesque in the doorway. He clapped and laughed, and she bowed.

"More," he said.

"No. Really, no." The sadness had crept in, like cold. The sadness that she didn't get to do it anymore, to dance with Jeremy, to be lifted by him into the air, as if she might fly.

Aidan nodded. "OK." They were speaking quietly—Bob was snoring. Aidan stood, careful not to disturb Bob as he moved, and raised his arms—then did his own arabesque, veering off balance; then holding it still.

This time Emily laughed.

Then she saw Aidan give a little shiver, the fire's warmth now fading. Was that pain in her chest love? She supposed it was.

She pulled him close, put her arms around him. She hadn't known, until he'd arrived, that she had always wanted him. Always wanted someone to love, to protect. Always.

"Are you scared?" she asked.

"No," he said.

"Really?"

He closed his eyes. "Why would I be?" he said. "You're with me."

He trusts me, she thought. It warmed her, everywhere, but at the same time it speared her heart with ice.

What if she couldn't save him?

What if she could—and he was gone, and she would never see him again?

Whatever happened, something would be taken from her.

She closed her eyes. She wasn't going to sleep—they could sleep, but not her. She needed to listen out for the men who would be coming after them.

CHAPTER 12

EMILY WAS IN the studio, on the springy wooden floor. She was dancing with Jeremy. *Swan Lake.*

They were alone, the lights low, night pressing dark at the windows. Practicing; always practicing. So that their movements would be perfect, so that their pain and tiredness would translate into grace.

They were alone, but it wasn't romantic, it was focused. He'd been in her gymnastics class—Emily's mom took her every Saturday morning. Jeremy's mom taught ballet, was once second soloist with the Chicago ballet. She'd seen Emily doing floorwork at the start of their class—the choreography in her routine, the leaps and spins—and told Emily's mom she had to join Jeremy's ballet lessons.

"She has talent," Jeremy's mom had said as they walked to the car afterward, past the Olive Garden, crisp Minnesotan air cooling the sweat on Emily's skin.

"Yes," said Emily's mom. "She's very strong. Flexible."

"No," said Jeremy's mom. "I mean, she can *dance.*"

Emily's mom made a face like she didn't understand. "We're not . . . um," she said. "My husband had to leave the army. Ballet sounds kind of expensive."

"I'll teach her for free," said Jeremy's mom. "If I didn't, it would be a crime."

That was why Emily was here, gliding with Jeremy across the floor, pirouetting, again and again, until it was right. His mom—Francesca—said she was good enough to audition for Chicago or even New York. Already she and Jeremy were going to exhibitions, dancing as a couple.

"Concentrate," said Jeremy as she slipped, went down on her knee.

"Sorry," she said. "Let's go again."

He put his arm around her, their fingers intertwined, both of them reaching up, and then he swung her out and around and she was spinning away from his touch—

Only, no, because the room dissolved around her, the floor fell away, and she was in freefall for a moment, until a hand was on her again, a proprietorial hand, not gentle like Jeremy's but squeezing her, squeezing her behind, a hand that said, you are mine. . . . She was in the corridor leading to the locker rooms, after the second game of the season, and Brad Mecklenburg, linebacker, was grabbing her and turning her to face him, grabbing her just above the line of her skirt, in a way that made her superconscious of how short it was, her stupid pleated cheerleader's skirt.

"Hey, Minnesota," he said.

"Hey, asshole," she said, pulling away from him.

Rain clouds crossed the blue sky of his eyes. Little muscles in his jaw twitched.

"Quit playing hard to get," he said.

"I'm not playing." She could still feel his fingers on her, though they weren't anymore. He had his arms crossed. There was a sheen of sweat on his forehead. His helmet swung from one hand.

She glanced around. There was no one. The corridor was empty. It was only afternoon, but the rectangle of outdoor air, behind them, was already black, the sun long since set, the stadium lights shooting down a shaft of sodium glow. She couldn't believe he was hassling her again.

"You're going to prom with me, Vasquez," said Brad.

"It's Perez, and no, I'm not," she said.

He laughed. "We'll see." He took a step toward her, smiling now, a smile she could tell he thought was charming, a smile she could tell he'd used before. "I usually get what I want," he said.

Emily was sure he did. Even Rachel, the cheerleading coach, seemed to think that was half of what they were there for. "Cheerleading teaches team spirit," she'd said. "And core strength and athleticism and discipline. It will look great on your college applications." And then she'd winked. "And, of course, it significantly raises your chances of getting a boyfriend on the football team and a *killer* date for prom."

The other girls had laughed.

Emily had not.

Now Brad took another step forward, put out his hands, and held her by the waist. Tight. Everyone else seemed to have left—it was as if the whole stadium was empty. She felt one hand move down, and he was so strong, and she tried to twist away from him because no—

This wasn't what had happened—

He'd sneered and walked off—that time anyway—

This wasn't her memory—

But then the corridor melted into blackness and cold and the texture of pine needles, all around her, and she heard Aidan call out her name in distress; someone was shaking her, the men from the government, and, "No, no, you can't have him, leave us alone, I swear to God I'll—" she shouted, but when she opened her eyes fully and let the light in, she saw it was Bob crouching over her.

The fire was low and smoking. Aidan was whimpering, curled into her side. His skin was near-blue with cold; he felt trembling and weak against her. Soft sunlight, coming through the branches above, made specks and sparkles on everything.

Bob held something in front of Emily's face. Something small and orange.

She peered at it. The SPOT tracker.

Oh.

CHAPTER 13

"WHAT'S THIS?" BOB said.

"It's a SPOT tracker."

"I know it's a SPOT tracker. It's *my* SPOT tracker. What I want to know is what it was doing in your goddamn pocket." He was sweating, despite the cold; pale-looking.

She looked down; touched her jeans. "You're frisking me now?"

She felt Aidan move in closer.

"I wanted to know why those men came after us with frickin' assault rifles. You said you'd explain, but I haven't heard any explanation coming out of your mouth." It was about the longest thing he'd said since they'd crashed.

"It's . . . hard to put into words. And anyway, you fell asleep as I was about to tell you. Last night."

He barked a short, unamused laugh. "You know we could have been rescued by now if I'd just pressed a button on this thing?"

"No," she said. "The men with assault rifles would just have come quicker."

A pause.

"Why? What did you do? I mean, apart from burning down the goddamn school."

She shook her head. "It was the stadium," she said. "Not even that. Not really. A locker room. And apart from that, *I* didn't do anything."

His forehead creased. "Someone else did?"

"Yeah."

"Your brother?"

"He didn't do anything, either."

"Then what?" asked Bob.

"I did do something," said Aidan quietly. "I existed."

"Aidan, you don't have to—"

"I think I do, probably," said Aidan, teeth chattering very lightly.

He was sitting now, hugging his knees to his chest, all vulnerable little boy, his skin so pale, and Emily wanted to grab hold of the rock beside her and pull it out like a concertina from the cliff and stretch it around him, cocoon him in stone, so nothing could ever harm him. To set light to the whole forest, to keep him warm.

Silly, really.

She reached out to bring him into a hug, but he shook his head.

Bob was looking between them, from one to the other, bemused. "Are you . . . were you . . . was someone hurting the kid?" he asked. "Your . . . f—" He shook his head. "Your family?"

Father, he'd been going to say.

"No," said Emily. "But they will hurt him if they catch him."

"Your family?"

"*No.* The men in black."

"White," said Bob.

"What? Oh. Yeah. Whatever."

Bob sat down heavily, still holding the SPOT tracker. "I really don't understand what's going on," he said.

Aidan sighed. A meaningful sigh.

Emily sent him a look: *You don't have to.*

He sent one back: *It's OK.*

That was the thing about looks. You could use them to speak with. They were a kind of universal communication. Emily liked that. She wasn't big on speaking. Her mom was always doing it— narrating everything. That wasn't Emily's style. She liked to find other ways to communicate. Her eyes. Dancing: the movement of her body through space.

Fire.

Though that had been kind of an accident, and totally Jeremy's fault.

OK, not really.

"I think," said Aidan, "I think I can show you."

Bob was watching him closely now.

Everything was very still. There was bright light outside the shelter; but inside, it was as if the moment before dawn persisted, everything dull and shadowy, gravid with the day about to be revealed. Everything shaded by the pine-needled branches.

Aidan closed his eyes; rippled with effort. She knew that what he did was a reflexive survival instinct; it was hard for him to override it like this.

Then his outlines, the silhouette made in space by his body, the actual boy shape of him, began to shimmer, to heat-haze, to blur.

CHAPTER 14

AIDAN MOVED OUTWARD from his own self, and his shape altered, became strange and hard to understand: hard to fit into your mind, because there were no containers, no boxes in there, in your mind, for him to go into, to be framed by, no references at all to pin him in place.

Part of the problem with understanding it, Emily thought, was that movies always used bits of animals to represent them: tentacles, bug eyes, that sort of thing. People could imagine only things that corresponded to their own world's physics, its biology, its system of structures. Whereas the reality was just . . . was just . . . something that you almost couldn't see, even, because you had never seen anything like it, were not equipped in any way to delineate it in vision.

Aidan had said, in her bedroom, soon after they met: "My real form does not fit into your ontology."

She'd had to look that one up.

Was there an impression of a head? Eyes? It was hard to tell. She remembered his ship, how she had known right away what it was—and not because it looked like any of the photos, like any of the movies. No: she had known because its corners had been in the wrong places, its edges had not made sense.

Bob was opening and closing his mouth, and he, at least, looked like an animal, like a fish dumbly kissing water, as he scrambled backward to the edge of the shelter.

Then Aidan—the thing that had been Aidan—retracted back inward, folded, a time-lapse video of origami, into the form of a little boy again.

There was a long silence.

"What. The— H-h-he's . . . an alien?" said Bob.

"Not at all," said Aidan. "I'm me. As far as I'm concerned, *you're* an alien."

That was when Bob passed out.

CHAPTER 15

EMILY CROUCHED OVER Bob. She didn't like having to tax his mind like this, with the strain of something so big—and now that she was close to him, she didn't like the heat that was coming from his skin, either, or the pallor of it.

She didn't like that at least two men with very large guns were probably close to their position, right now, drawn by the thinning smoke from their dying fire, and Bob was unconscious.

How long would it have taken to traverse that snow plain they'd surfed down on their plane wing? A couple of hours? If anything, the men should be here already, which meant they might well be outside, waiting for them to make a move. Either that or they were regrouping at the crash site, taking things slow. Being cautious, believing she still had the gun.

Whatever: they knew that they were chasing an injured man and two kids. They wouldn't be worried. Like good hunters, they could take their time.

Emily didn't like any of this.

When the pilot opened his eyes, she helped him to sit up. He kept glancing over at Aidan, who was sitting very quietly.

"I'm feverish," Bob said. "I must be hallucinating." He was touching his arm, where the skin was red and mottled.

"You're feverish," she said. "Yes. But you're not hallucinating."

"But . . . but . . ."

Emily didn't have time for this. None of them had time for it. She explained it all, as succinctly as she could. How she had found the ship—not that *ship* was the right word, of course. It had been the day she'd been suspended from school, but she didn't mention that part to Bob.

The rest, though, she told. How she had heard it first—the breaking of the trees, the impact with the earth. She'd run out of the house a moment before, after her mom drove her home, after the boys' locker room burned, and her mom was shouting after her, shouting for her to come back, that her dad was going to be home soon, that they needed to talk about this as a family.

And then there had been the noise: splintering branches; a dull thud.

She had gone out from their yard on the edge of the small town by the lake and into the woods, and she told Bob how she had seen the thing there in the burned and blackened earth, all the snow melted into air. The near impossibility of comprehending the angles and lines her eyes were delivering to her brain.

And then the creature: the small creature, weakened, that came out. Too weak, she learned afterward, to put up its instinctual defense, to hide itself within the form of what she would need to keep safe, to protect.

Emily hadn't known what to do. She could barely understand where this thing's edges were, let alone offer any kind of help, of healing.

But then, gradually, it had taken on the form of a boy.

The boy touched her hand, closed his eyes, and stood there for a long moment, in a shaft of light slanting down through the trees.

She said the same thing as Bob. The a-word.

The little boy opened his eyes and looked up at her. "I suppose," he said. "But please don't tell? Until I can get home again . . ."

"Don't tell?" she said. "There's a ship. There's *you* . . ."

He shook his head. "There's only a little boy, lost. We'll hide the ship."

This was all going too fast. She looked around, remembering the . . . whatever it was that she had seen. His real body. "Won't someone find out?" she had asked. "Won't they see . . . what I saw? The real you?"

"No, not if you keep my secret. No one else will. They will only see"—he indicated his boy's body—"this. Or something similar. I was . . . weak . . . when you found me. That's why you saw me as I really am. Now it is working again."

"What's working?"

"What I do," he said. "I can't help it. It's . . . it's . . ." He touched her hand again. She had a strange thought that there was something more than gestural about it. Like he was taking something from her. But not in a bad way. "It's like a squid spraying ink."

"What do you do?"

"I make myself into something small, if I encounter another species. Something they will love. Something they will protect."

And she looked down at the small boy, who was staring up at her with such hope and trust. And something inside her shifted.

"Yes," she said. "I see that."

"Only . . . it won't totally work on you. I mean, you'll see me as a human. But because you saw the . . . other . . . me, you'll always remember. You'll always know who I really am."

"Um," she said. "OK." This whole thing was so baffling, so new, that she didn't know how to respond to any of it; didn't know how she felt, even.

"Do you live with other people?"

She thought of her parents, who would be wondering where she was, who would be wanting to talk about why she was no longer allowed to go to school, about why the police were considering pressing charges for arson.

"Yes," she said.

"Then they . . . People who haven't seen my true form . . . will see me as someone they already know. They will think they've always known me."

"OK," she said. She hadn't realized the significance of that at the time.

"Emily," he said.

She hadn't mentioned her name.

She took in a breath. Glanced at her hand where he had touched it. "What did you do when you touched me then?"

"I saw your memories. Everything you know."

"Oh." She turned her hand over, marveling. It felt the same. She didn't even feel scared.

"Emily, will you keep my secret? I have to find a way to get home. . . . No one can know my real self. Or they won't let me leave. Will you help me?"

She didn't hesitate. The wanting-to-protect thing was already working. "Yes," she said.

So they covered the ship with branches, and they went back to the house, and that was when things got weird—which was in itself a weird thing to think, given what had already happened.

When she was small, Emily had always wanted a little brother or sister, someone to play with. Someone to hang out with, have a shared language with, songs to sing, jokes. But her parents had always said no.

"We've got a perfect kid," her dad would say. "Why would we need another?"

Which shouldn't have been annoying but was. Emily didn't want to be perfect: she just didn't want to be alone, to be lonely, to be always different from the people around her. She didn't know how to tell her parents that she didn't *like* the same things as them: hiking, camping, the great outdoors.

But she did know one thing: *they* liked those things, and they liked Alaska, and they definitely didn't want any other kids—as far as they were concerned, life was perfect as it was.

"We want to give you everything," her mom always said—but *everything* didn't include a sibling.

So it was a surprise when she walked in with Aidan—thinking she would sneak him up to her room and bring him some food before the shit really hit the fan—it was a thin plan, flimsy, but it was all she had—and when she entered the kitchen, at first their faces were dark and her dad opened his mouth to shout at her, and then he saw Aidan, and beamed, and clapped him on the back and said, "Aidan! We wondered where you'd gone, but you were out with your big sister, huh?" and her mom gave the little boy a kiss on the cheek and mussed his hair.

CHAPTER 16

BACK THEN, THE day he arrived, Emily looked wide-eyed at the alien who was now a boy, who was now Aidan.

He shrugged.

"I can't help it," he said.

"Help what, honey?" said Mom.

"Being so intelligent," said Aidan. "We were doing riddles, and I figured out Emily's easy." He did a kind of eye-roll thing, directed at her. A way of including her, as if they were a team, as if it were them against everyone else, as if they were *complicit*. In that moment, Emily sensed her heart could go one way or another, she could accept or reject what was being offered; but she smiled at him. She was like him; she couldn't help it.

Then her parents turned to her.

"Aidan, go to your room," her dad said. As if Aidan had a room.

"Why?" said Aidan.

"We need to talk to Emily. About . . . what happened at school."

Her dad pointed to the chairs at the kitchen table, like: *Sit down.* Emily sat.

"A *fire,* Emily?" he said. "What were you thinking? I mean, I knew you didn't love this place, but what the . . . ?"

She shrugged.

"The school is considering full expulsion," said her mom. "And the police want to talk to you." She paused, her voice crumbling. "Is it something I did? Or didn't do? Am I to blame for this somehow?" Tears started in her eyes.

"No, sweetheart, this isn't on you," said Emily's dad, putting an arm around her mom. "Emily. See what you're doing to your mother."

Emily looked down at the table. At the whorls and swirls in the wood. What could she say? She'd burned down part of the *school.* She hadn't meant to, but that sort of distinction didn't feel like it would improve anything. This was about as bad as it got.

She looked up and met Aidan's eyes.

He winked.

Then he turned to her parents, and . . .

It was hard to describe. He just sort of looked at them, but he was glowing. Only without actually glowing.

Her mom opened and closed her mouth, like a nutcracker soldier. Her dad leaned his head over to one side.

"What were we talking about?" said her mom.

"I . . . I don't know," said her dad.

"Huh," said her mom. "It's the strangest thing. . . . I just . . . I . . ."

"You said we could stream a movie tonight," said Aidan. "Make popcorn."

Her mom's face brightened. "Yes! Good idea, honey."

"Emily can choose," said Aidan. "She's had a tough day." He smiled at her.

"Sure," said her dad. "You've always been so generous, kiddo." *Always been.*

Head spinning, Emily took Aidan's hand and led him upstairs to her room, leaving her parents standing in the kitchen, bemused looks on their faces.

"Whatever you did to them," she said when they were in her room, "don't ever do it to me."

Aidan nodded. "OK."

"Promise?"

"I promise."

She sighed. "It won't work forever, making it go away. I could have burned down the whole football stadium."

"It'll work for however long I want it to," he replied. Then he smiled his brightest smile. "Anyway, I know all your memories, remember? I know you didn't mean to do it."

Later, they came into the kitchen for dinner, ahead of their movie night. Emily's mom had made hot dogs, and was popping corn in a big pan on the stovetop. Emily hated the kitchen. It was small and functional, no decoration apart from her mom's motivational fridge magnets.

A picture of an arctic fox cub, with the words: WE ALL HAVE THE POTENTIAL FOR GREATNESS WITHIN US.

Another with a flexed bicep and: BE STRONGER THAN YOUR EXCUSES.

And one her mom loved so much there were actually two

magnets with the same words: YOU DON'T KNOW YOUR OWN STRENGTH.

Her mom had set the table earlier, and now she frowned at it, like it had moved when her back was turned. "Huh," she said. "I'm such a ditz. I set the table for three." She went over to the cupboards and took out an extra plate, knife and fork, glass.

If it hadn't been so freaky, it would have been impressive. There were no photos of Aidan in the house, only of Emily, but it didn't seem to matter to her parents. He had always been there. He would always be there.

When they went up to bed that night, her parents somehow didn't see that the spare room didn't have any stuff in it—that it was just a double bed and a lamp on a small table, ready for guests. They did not appear to notice that there were no toys, no posters, no crayon marks on the walls. They tucked Aidan in and told him a bedtime story—Emily watched and listened from the doorway; it was about a boy who climbed a mountain to look for a flower that would save his grandmother, and never had she been told a story like it.

It was *weird*. It was awful, it was sad. All she had ever wanted was for her parents to leave her alone, but in that moment she felt a deep pang of jealousy.

But she never resented him. In fact, he made her laugh, just like their parents said—*their* parents, their parents, it was even in her own head.

He teased her; made up silly songs about farts and kangaroos; played long and elaborate games of Monopoly with her, the rules of the game only vaguely applying to the baroque world they created together, of landlords and tenants and anarchists and magicians.

From that first day she knew: she would never let anything happen to him. He'd looked inside her head—he knew everything about her, all her secrets. He was someone she couldn't lie to, and she'd loved him almost instantly.

She should have known it couldn't last.

CHAPTER 17

THEY WERE ON their way to school; Aidan was in third grade, he always had been. Mrs. Jameson was his teacher, and she liked him, though he was hard to teach and often acted up.

Well, *Aidan* was on his way to school. Emily was taking Aidan, more precisely. She herself was still suspended, pending a police investigation—not that she had spoken much to her parents about it since the first blowup with her mom when she'd picked Emily up from the school—after Miss Brady caught her outside, with the lighter and cigarettes, in the parking lot, where the snow was melting from the heat of the fire.

Aidan had derailed everything.

Even the investigation: two police detectives had come to the door. (Emily had a feeling there *were* only two police officers in the town.) They'd asked to speak to Emily about the suspected arson, and Aidan had stepped out of the living room and looked at them, and they had gone away, frowning and muttering something about a lost dog.

But that, in a weird way, was good. Emily had done something terrible, something irreparable, and yet she existed in a bubble inside reality, a bubble where it didn't matter, where no one close to her seemed to remember it in detail, and there were no repercussions, despite the blackened metal beams where the roof of the locker room had been.

Her parents *knew* it had happened, their memory had returned enough for that, but they weren't angry about it, despite people in town treating them weirdly because of it—it was as if Aidan had done something to take the oxygen from the flames of their anger, starve it.

So she lived in a strange limbo. Still suspended but facing no other consequences for her mistake. With a brother who had always existed but didn't exist.

Aidan had his own mythology, Emily had quickly realized. His own place and story within the family. He was cheeky, he was funny: that was his thing. Emily's dad reminded her, on another day a week or so later, how even when Aidan was a toddler, he had bossed everyone around. How if he or her mom had annoyed Aidan when he was, like, three years old, he would say, "Hey, stop that, or I will throw you in the trash." But with a twinkle, so you had to laugh.

He'd been affectionate too, always: her mom and dad agreed on that. Her mom told her how once she'd been going out to get a haircut and Emily was going to babysit Aidan. He'd been four, no more. Still tiny: just over waist-high. Mom had been at the door, coat on, and he'd glared at her. "Mommy," he'd said. "You can't go without giving me a duddle." He had been unable to say *k* sounds, so the car was the *tar* and a cuddle was a *duddle*.

Except that he had been unable to say anything because he didn't exist.

He was built by their minds.

He was a thing out of place and time, a strange gift from the sky, and for the first time Emily had an ally, someone who understood her, and a loud, fun family, and not only that but protection from her own stupid mistake.

For the first time in a long time, she was *happy*.

But then the men in black had come.

They'd been passing Java Jamboree, the only coffee shop in town. Emily felt Aidan's hand tighten in hers. There were two men in suits inside, looking back at them through the window. They were wearing sunglasses, though it was dark even in the morning.

"Those men," Aidan said. "They see me."

"Yeah," she said, distracted. "Hard not to." She'd bought him a jacket, for warmth, but her allowance only went so far and most of his clothes were still hers. Today, he was wearing her old bright pink coat with a dinosaur on it, and neon-green pants. She'd brought them down from the attic, where her outgrown things were stored. Strange, the way her parents kept all this too-small stuff, all her old onesies and things, even though they didn't want a bigger family.

Hadn't wanted a bigger family. Because they seemed super-happy to have Aidan: her dad was always taking him out to play catch, and throwing him up in the air and making him giggle, and the part of Emily that she kept hidden, even from herself, was a blade of jealousy turned inward on her own stomach, lacerating it.

"No," he said. "They see *me*. They know who I am."

It switched her out of idle and into drive. Her eyes flicked over to the men in the window. Their out-of-town suits. *City* suits. Their close-cropped military hair. Her dad's hair had been like that when he came out of the army.

"What do they want?" she said. But she had an idea that she already knew. People always wanted to take things apart to understand them, didn't they? As if a thing couldn't be understood by leaving it whole.

"Nothing good," he said.

After that day, they saw the men everywhere. It was a small town. And one day the men knocked on the door, and Emily and Aidan hid upstairs, and only came down when they had gone.

"Some kind of census," said Emily's mom. "They wanted to see you, but I told them you were asleep." She looked at her watch, and her mouth turned down, a line of puzzlement. "Not sure why I said that. I mean, you haven't napped in the daytime for years, Aidan."

Aidan tapped his head and winked at Emily.

But they knew the men would be back, so that was when they decided to leave. It solved everything: get Aidan away from these men who wanted to take him somewhere, to experiment on him—at least that was what they assumed. Get Emily away from the town where, at some point, people were going to remember that she had torched the fricking boys' locker room.

Her *parents* would at some point remember.

So they'd packed some stuff, and they'd stowed away on the little plane, climbing aboard with the mail packages and the supplies while Bob was having coffee with the two-man ground crew. Security was more or less nonexistent at the airfield, and what little there was, Aidan had bypassed with his mind tricks.

They were gone—they were mist—they were out of there.

Until the plane crashed.

CHAPTER 18

"AND THAT, BASICALLY, is that," said Emily to Bob.

Bob seemed a little less agitated, but he was still sweating, still an unhealthy color.

"Jesus Christ," he said.

Emily's dad had washed her mouth out with actual soap and water once when she was seven and blasphemed like that, having heard it at school. He was a Methodist, on top of all that military discipline. They all were.

Even Aidan. Ha-ha.

"And now those men are still coming," said Emily. "I figure they traced your radio distress signal. So we need to go. Sorry. I know it's a lot to take in."

A hollow laugh from Bob. He started to rise but fell down. Emily had to prop him up. "Let's go, then," he said. "I mean, none of this makes sense, but we have to keep going, right?"

"You posit a good life philosophy," said Aidan.

"Don't talk like that," said Bob. "Not with that face. It creeps me out." He paused. "Wait." He turned to Emily. "You said he can't help it. Making people see him as . . . as a kid or whatever. But . . ." He scratched his head. "I mean, it's not totally working on me now, is it? I see a kid, but I *know* he's not one. If you get me."

"Once you know," said Aidan. "You know. You can't unknow it. Like Emily. And the men in black, as she calls them."

"OK." Another pause. "But . . . what are you doing here? On Earth, I mean?"

Emily turned to Aidan too, curious.

Bob stared at her. "You never *asked* him?"

"No. I just . . . It never occurred to me."

"Jesus," said Bob. "You kids."

Aidan nodded, though. They had started walking through the forest, away from the crash site. In the rough direction of the cabin by the lake. Emily was hoping there was some food there, some sort of supplies. Her stomach was fizzing with hunger.

"It's a fair question," he said.

"You bet your ass it's a fair question," said Bob.

Aidan smiled. "We are here to observe. To protect, you might say. We hope you might avoid some of our mistakes. One thing about my physical appearance is true, though: I am young. Not so young as Aidan, in relative terms. But still a child. When I crashed, when I became . . . lost . . . I don't know. I wanted to see Earth up close. The creatures. But I was not very good with the craft yet, and I got too close and crashed. You could think of me as a kid who lets go of their parent's hand in a supermarket, and turns, and is alone."

"You don't talk like a child who's lost in a supermarket," said Bob.

"The analogy is not perfect," said Aidan, "I admit. But it contains some truth."

"Like?"

"Like he has to get back to his parents," Emily said. "They'll be worried about him. They miss him. And he misses them."

"Oh, you knew *that* part?" said Bob.

"Yeah," she said. "It was the only part that seemed to matter. That's why we're here. To get to where we can find him help."

Bob sent his eyes heavenward, to the slivers of lightening sky showing through the trees. "So where *are* you going?"

"To a place where we can send them a message," said Emily. "His family. His real family, I mean." She felt a twinge of pain at that, of sadness. All of this was about getting him home, but that meant losing him, and she wanted him to be back with the ones who loved him, and also she loved him and didn't want him to be gone.

As if two forces were trying to tear her heart apart.

"Good Lord," said Bob. "The kids are in charge, and our mission is some kind of E.T. shit. I may never get out of this alive." He was stepping heavily over the stones and roots underfoot, his balance wobbly.

Emily looked at the sheen of his forehead. On the exposed skin of his wrist, she saw thin red lines, branching, his blood vessels brightly visible against the paleness.

No, she thought. *No, you may not.*

The thought made her sadder than she would have expected not long before.

CHAPTER 19

EMILY HAD TO support Bob as they headed down the valley. It was a long slope, a cliff on their left side and rocky scree on the other, leading down to a series of foothills and then the pair of lakes. Bob was wincing as he walked, one forearm over Emily's shoulder, for balance.

Emily glanced behind. She thought she caught movement high on the hills they had come down from. A figure, maybe, stepping behind a tree. Or it may have been her imagination, or a trick of the light.

Yeah.

Or it was men with guns coming for them. She wondered again why they hadn't caught up by now. But then, they only had to keep their distance, and wait. This landscape was not hospitable.

She shivered involuntarily.

Aidan walked ahead—if someone tracked them from behind, it would give him another second or two, and that could save him. It was a clear day. Far away in front of them, on the hills overlooking the upper lake, Emily could see a couple of caribou making their way through a stand of low trees. *Too* far away, even if she'd had a rifle. Her stomach rumbled so loud she felt it could be heard, echoing against rock.

"Is this the right way?" Emily asked Aidan quietly.

"To the HAARP facility? Roughly." That was where they needed to go to get Aidan home. To send him away.

"How far is it?" she asked.

"Far."

"Can we make it?"

Aidan glanced at Bob. "Not all of us, I don't think."

A little later, Bob went down on one knee, swore, and got up again. They paused. An eagle rode a thermal high above them. Emily would have been interested, usually, but barely glanced at it. She was more worried about the veins sticking out on Bob's forehead.

"Sorry," said Emily. "Sorry for all of this."

Bob glanced at Aidan. "All you did was find him," he said eventually. With half his usual gruffness. "If it hadn't been you, it would have been someone else. Someone less kind, maybe."

"No. I mean, the SPOT tracker. If I hadn't taken it, if I'd—"

"Then they'd just have got to us quicker, like you said. Maybe in the night, when we were sleeping, that first night after we . . . after I . . . crashed. They'd have found us, and Aidan . . . Aidan would have been lost."

She nodded. This was probably true. But still: the pilot was shivering, and his blood had soaked through the T-shirt sleeve she'd tied around his arm, and there were dark crescents under his eyes. The sun was low in the sky. The sun was nearly always low in the sky up here.

"Maybe someone else might have come," she said. "Someone who would have rescued us." She swallowed. "Then you wouldn't have got shot. I mean, I wouldn't have got you shot."

Aidan cleared his throat; she thought he might say something, but he didn't. They walked on in silence for a moment. Bob kept putting his hand on Emily's shoulder for support. But he was pretending like he wasn't doing it, kind of, so she was always careful not to meet his eye.

"You don't always get to choose who finds you," he said with a grimace.

"Huh," said Emily. She wasn't sure if he meant that in an angry way or a nice way, and she didn't really want to ask. Maybe it was both.

"We don't work as a team, we die," said Bob. "We'll get out of these mountains, and then . . ." He trailed off, the implication clear.

"Then we're on our own?"

"Uh-huh," he said, nodding. "I don't want to get tangled up in your shit any more than I have to. You can call your parents or something."

"Hmm," said Emily.

He watched her face. "You don't think they'll be looking for you?"

"No, I do." In fact, she could very easily imagine her father and mother trekking through the snow, backpacks on, in layered clothing, carrying compasses and water and knives. Like when they used to go camping—hiking for days through the Rockies or the Adirondacks. "I just . . . I don't know if I want them to find me."

"Like I said, we don't always get to choose," said Bob. He walked in silence for a moment. "What's so bad about them anyway?"

"There's nothing *obviously* bad about them," said Emily. "They're just . . . different. Intense. My dad, I guess he never got over busting his knee and having to leave the army. Sometimes I think I'm like his mini-me, and he wants me strong because he can't be, totally. Or whatever. And my mom . . . she's just, like, a bunch of clichés about work and teams and stuff. She doesn't . . . she doesn't get me."

She doesn't understand dancing.

She doesn't understand what art *is*.

Bob was looking at her. "Longest thing I've heard you say." An echo: she'd thought a similar thing about him.

She shrugged. "Plus," she said, "they made us move here." She glanced at him. He wouldn't have become a bush pilot if he hadn't loved Alaska. "No offense," she added.

He grunted.

She could have said:

They're tent pegs and engines and screws and knots and mindfulness and homemade granola and inspirational posters. They're short days with no light. They're a place with one store with a few paperbacks on a rack, which they call a library, and they don't mind any of that—they like it, they want to be in the middle of nowhere.

"We want to give you everything."

But what if she didn't need any of it? What if what she needed was a different life altogether?

"What do they do?" asked Bob, though she guessed he must know; it was a small town, after all, and he was the de facto mailman. He was clearly making conversation to keep them going, to keep himself going.

"My dad teaches shop at the school," she said. "My mom helps out at the general store sometimes, and she's always jogging around town. You must know her."

"Gray hair? A little . . . severe?"

"Yep."

"I know her. Pioneer type. A woman out of her time."

Emily was surprised at that: it was good, and true, and perceptive. "Yeah," she said. "They're . . . outdoorsy. When I was a kid in Minnesota, we spent more time in tents than in the house. National parks, the Adirondacks, the Rockies. When we weren't in church."

He gestured at the mountains around them. "You're in your element, then," he said.

"No," she said. "In theirs."

"Fine. So what do *you* want?"

She didn't say anything to that, just shrugged.

"OK," said Bob. "Air of mystery. I can respect that."

His words were coming out with a wheeze. He stopped to get his breath and shielded his eyes from the sun, looking around. They had come nearly to the end of the valley, a few hundred yards from the trees, the cliff on their left—Emily didn't know if it was a thin, knife-edge ridge or a thick bluff—coming to an end. She didn't know what was on the other side.

"Shit," Bob said. He pointed, back the way they had come.

Emily turned and saw a white figure—no, two white figures—making their way down the valley above them. Within firing distance, if they had telescopic sights, which surely they did.

Yes—she saw the rifles now, long black lines against their bodies. There wasn't much black on the mountainside, so they stood out.

Oh, she thought.

Oh, no.

CHAPTER 20

EMILY SCANNED THEIR surroundings: no shelter, no cover.

Of course not.

Just snow, and the trees too far to run for. They could take cover behind the cliff, maybe, though first they'd have to get to the end of it, and find out what was below it—here, it was just a wall hemming them in. But at the end, there might be a sheer drop.

Something zipped overhead, followed—confusingly—by a pop like a firework going off.

Emily yanked Aidan down hard; Bob was already on his knees, though she didn't know if he'd done that deliberately or fallen. Behind them, up the mountain, she saw the first white figure raise the rifle again. There was another, a little way behind. Two. The other must not have survived the blast from the helicopter that had punched him to the ground. A part of her was glad of that. A part of her was very definitely not. That part of her felt sick.

She moved in front of Aidan, pushed him behind her. "Run!" she said. "Run downhill!"

And then she started running up the slope, away from him, jagging left and right. It was instinctual, almost, the only thing she could think to do: make herself a bigger target, give Aidan time to get away. Maybe even avoid the bullets until she could get close enough to . . . what? Well, she'd come to that. She had:

Fists, teeth, forehead, fingernails.

Though, of course, they had guns, so it was all academic, really. But time. Time, she could give him.

Zip. Another bullet, whipping past her right side, so close she felt its slipstream. Then the bang.

What the hell was she doing? Was she really risking her life for someone who wasn't even a real person? Yes. Apparently, she was.

And then:

A rumble from farther up the mountain. She was still moving, still dodging sideways, but her eyes were on the snow at the top of the valley, which was starting to move, to shift, to flow downward—as if the mountain was turning to liquid, was melting. The two men in white turned too, guns falling by their sides, and then they were running toward her, away from the rushing avalanche.

She spun around. "Avalanche!" she shouted to Bob and Aidan as she ran back to them, a pointless warning, given they could surely see the mass of snow heading down the mountain toward them.

She was on them now—she grabbed Aidan's hand and pulled him toward the shadow of the overhang. To the end of the cliff, she was thinking. To the end, and then left, and hope it's not just a drop—hope there's some kind of plateau there to stand on. Bob was limping along behind, not fast, but she had to be practical. She couldn't carry him.

Aidan slipped, went down, and she dragged him a little without meaning to—she was holding his hand, his body spinning. She dropped to one knee, picked him up, and threw him over one shoulder: fireman's carry. She glanced back at Bob, who was gaining now. Her eyes were drawn to the avalanche itself. The first man, the lower one, was running fast, or as fast as he could in the powdery snow.

So was the other one, but he was higher up, and it was too late. She saw him fall forward, as if thrown, as if pushed in the back, and then the white engulfed him, roaring now as it gathered speed and force.

One down, a detached part of her mind thought.

Then: the rock to their left came to an end, and below it, yes, below it was a kind of wide ledge, and below that a deep ravine— but the ledge, the ledge was the important thing.

She rounded the corner, and then it was stopping her momentum that was the problem: she planted her feet, skidding as if on skis, dropping Aidan at the same time as if he were ballast. She came to a stop with one leg dangling over the ravine. She lowered her face to the cold, icy ground, and breathed out. She needed to get up, to bring her whole body onto firm ground, but for now she was unable to move; she dug her fingers into the cold rock and held still. She wasn't safe yet, but she wasn't dead, either.

She looked up. Bob had got there just in time: he stood, holding on to the rock face as the leading edge of the avalanche poured past and down the valley they had just been in, roaring as it went, a deluge of snow—but they were untouched by it, protected by the wall of rock.

Bob saw her, and came over, and gave her his hand. He grunted with pain as he pulled her up, but he did it: she was on the ledge, rock under her feet.

"Thanks," she said.

"Thank *you*," said Aidan, coming to stand with her. "You saved me." He was looking at her with wide eyes.

"What else was I going to do?" she said.

He smiled.

Then:

"Don't move," said a voice behind them. A man's voice.

Emily turned, and there was an assault rifle aimed at her head.

"Try anything and I'll shoot," he said.

CHAPTER 21

KEEP CALM AND **CHEER.**

It was crazy, but those were the words that rang in Emily's head as she stared down the barrel of the gun.

It was crazy too that she was almost certainly about to die; impossible. That a man might simply shoot her on a mountainside.

It was crazy that she was going to die without seeing her parents again. Without telling them she loved them.

She still blamed them, of course, for making her move here. For replacing Jeremy and dance with loneliness and cheerleading. In theory. But it was getting harder and harder to hold on to that anger. To make it pulse inside her. Part of it had to do with Aidan. Part of it was just . . . tiredness.

And all of it, with that rifle pointed at her head, just seemed so pointless. All the anger. All the trouble at the school.

She hadn't *meant* to burn down the locker room—Miss Brady had just assumed.

It was all because of the cheerleading.

She hadn't wanted to do it—but the school didn't offer any

dance classes, so cheerleading was the closest thing. Her mom had been ecstatic, of course, when Emily said she was trying out: she talked about "spirit" and pride and teamwork, and said it would be good for Emily's social life and college applications. And Emily had done gymnastics, hadn't she? And enjoyed it?

Yeah. But she'd stopped when Jeremy's mom introduced her to ballet. Not that there was any point discussing it with her own mom. The woman would never understand.

The tryouts were straightforward: Emily did a cartwheel into a backflip, and that was basically it; she was light enough that they made her the flyer from the start—her job to be lifted into the air by three of the backstop team, spun, turned, thrown, and caught.

It was, to begin with, not entirely unlike dance. There were routines to learn, choreography. The girls were sweet too—mostly—even if some of them cared far too much about getting the best footballer boyfriend and the best yearbook photo. Still, none of what happened was on them.

It was never quite Emily's world—always more her mother's. Even the posters her mother would have loved. In the locker room they were everywhere. One read: KEEP CALM AND CHEER.

Emily thought that was a bit of a contradiction.

No, it just wasn't her thing, though she tried to go along with it, for the sake of *trying* to fit in.

But the boys.

The boys: it *was* on them, what happened.

Her first game, cheerleading, was on a Friday afternoon, against the Wolverines. Emily's team were the Bears.

She was surprised by the scale of the whole thing, considering the size of the town. The stadium had seemed outsized when they first arrived, but it soon filled up. Everywhere was that festival smell of popcorn and hot dogs. The crowd was raucous: kids from the school but also their parents, and even people who had nothing to do with the school at all. Emily's mom waved at her from the back row.

On the sidelines, she and her cheerleading squad went through the routines. Hush of their shoes against the Astroturf. Smell of burgers and onions and fireworks. All the time, Emily was conscious that the cheerleader uniform skirt barely covered her thighs, that the Lycra shorts underneath were uncomfortably tight. Of the eyes of boys and men in the crowd, and of how that was the point, really, when you got right down to it.

She and the other cheerleaders chanted:

Hard as ice,
Cold as snow,
We'll score high and you'll score low.

And they stunted: at halftime Emily was thrust upright into the cold air, balancing on Jen Dooley's, Marsha Kitteridge's, and Brittany Kozubek's hands. She threw up one leg to catch her foot, pulled it behind her head, and then kicked out, and—with a push from her teammates—finally rose into the air and corkscrewed, flipped, before landing on the flexing forearms of the girls.

"Good job!" said Brittany, and "Awesome stunting!" said Marsha, and Emily felt a warm glow.

"Hey, Perez," said call-me-Rachel, the coach, after the game— the Bears had lost by ten points. "You did super out there."

"Thanks," she'd said.

Then, on the way past the bleachers, through the wide concrete corridor, they'd passed a group of boys who were singing loud fight songs—and they stopped their singing and wolf-whistled and catcalled instead—and wasn't it funny, Emily thought now as she waited for the man in white to shoot her with his rifle, how both of those words had the names of animals in them?

One of the boys reached out, as they passed, and patted her ass.

She turned. "Hey."

Three of them lifted their hands; mock surrender and apology, eyes wide and laughing. "What?" they said.

"Touch me again and—"

"And what?" said one of the boys. Brad. Of course it was Brad. He was a sophomore, she'd bumped into him in the library, where he'd made a comment about her top. He was that kind of guy.

"And *what*?" Brad repeated.

And nothing, it turned out. She didn't know how to complete the sentence. And anyway, call-me-Rachel was ushering them on, toward the locker room.

"One of those guys touched me," Emily said as they changed out of their uniforms.

Rachel shrugged. "Goes with the territory."

The hell it does, thought Emily. But she didn't say anything. Still: rage was bubbling inside her; the uncompleted angry thought of her broken-off sentence to the guy, left inside her like a splinter, to fester.

To bring about everything bad that had happened since.

But then Aidan had turned up, and it was like none of that mattered anymore.

She just had to get him to safety.

And now the men had him—the man had him—the man with the gun, pointed at Emily.

She stood there, with the cliff beside her, and the drop on the other side, and the rifle's barrel huge in front of her, a hole leading to the end of the world.

She didn't care that she had failed—she was used to that. But she'd failed *Aidan*. And that was something she couldn't forgive—even of herself.

In her head, those four meaningless words echoed: KEEP CALM AND CHEER.

It was impossible; it was paralysis: because the one canceled out the other.

All she could do was stand there, entirely still.

CHAPTER 22

ALL OF THAT went through Emily's mind in a second, and the gun was still pointing at her, and she was still standing, unmoving. The human mind: it was like fairyland; time passed differently there. All these thoughts, ticker-taping across the inside of her head, and only an instant had gone by.

The man behind the gun—soldier? agent?—was wearing some kind of balaclava, so Emily could see only his brown eyes. They were flat, hard. His clothing—uniform?—was more suited to the cold than anything she was wearing. Warm ski jacket and pants, gloves.

He looked like someone who had killed people and would not hesitate to do so again.

"Hand over the . . . boy," he said. "And you can go."

Emily didn't think that was true. Then again, maybe it was. What would anyone say, after all, if she and Bob wandered into a small town somewhere in southwest Alaska and said they'd survived a plane crash with an alien boy but a man with a gun had taken him?

People would say they were crazy—it was obvious. That they'd suffered some kind of psychosis, brought about by the crash, by the cold, by the hunger.

So maybe the man really did intend to let them live. It was nice to think so anyway.

To her surprise, Bob limped in front of her, between her and the gun.

"You'll have to go through me first," he said to the man.

What?

The assault rifle remained steady. The man holding it cocked his head, as if considering.

"OK," he said. He raised the rifle a fraction.

"No—" began Aidan, pushing past Emily too, but there was a flicker of movement from the cliff wall, a shadow, dark liquid rock taking form, and—

Bear, realized Emily, and she could only watch, a spectator behind her own eyes, as the huge brown creature charged along the ledge, then up on its hind legs, paws coming down at the man-soldier-agent's head, and he raised his hands, screaming—at least Emily thought he was screaming, it might have been someone else—and he stepped back, and his heel went over the edge of the ravine, and that was it.

His weight toppled him backward, and he fired a volley of shots into the air—*dum-dum-dum*—as he flipped over, smashing his head on the rock, and then tumbling floppily down the chasm, a Ken doll turning end over end, making awful noises.

Emily was horrified: that was the word, *horrified.* She knew she should have been pleased—he'd been about to shoot her, she was sure of it—but she wasn't. It was something she had never seen before, a violence worse, somehow, than what had happened at the plane, perhaps because of the sounds and the way his body snapped and twisted. So sudden; so appalling. He was, she imagined, just doing his job, the man with the gun. And now he was bent in ways she didn't want to look too long at, far below them.

She wasn't, though, so horrified that she didn't notice, for a fraction, a scintilla of an instant, the rifle lying on the rock beside the man's body. Or the place, a little farther down, where the snowy loam hung over the ravine, and it would be possible— just—to jump down and recover the gun. She was her father's daughter, for better or worse.

But right now, there was the bear.

She turned, and the huge animal was motionless for a moment, paws up, claws the size of her thumbs. It was as tall as a bungalow. Bob too was standing very still.

Their eyes met. Hers and the bear's. Then hers and Bob's.

What do we do? hers said.

It really was amazing how much eyes could say.

I have no fucking idea, Bob's said.

Bottomless blackness of instinct and hunger: that was all the bear's eyes said.

CHAPTER 23

EMILY HAD READ kids' books in which people felt all kinds of primal connections when meeting animals, but she felt no kinship or convergence with this . . . thing. It was just murder on paws. Elemental. Something of the mountain that intended her to end. Cold, killing snow with a pulse.

Again, only a moment had passed.

Then Aidan took a step forward. Bob started to say something, but Aidan raised his hand to shush him. The bear's eyes tracked the little boy as he approached.

Soon, Aidan was standing right in front of the bear. It was like . . . Emily's mind grasped for something, some comparison, but there was none. It was like a tiny boy facing an enormous bear. He held out his hand and touched the bear's fur.

Then Aidan kind of *flickered.*

He went down on his hands and knees, a boy on all fours. Except that Emily didn't think he seemed like that, looked like that, to the bear. She thought he probably looked like a cub.

Because the next thing that happened was that the bear—it

was a female, Emily suddenly understood—hunkered down gently and licked Aidan's face. He laughed. The bear did a low growl that was somehow friendly, or at least not threatening, then rolled him onto his back—carefully, controlling its strength—and nuzzled his tummy. Aidan giggled.

Bob looked at Emily. His eyes said:

WTF?

She looked back. Hers said: *I give up on understanding any of this.* She helped her eyes out with a shrug of her shoulders—eyes can say a lot, but they sometimes need some backup.

Aidan was gazing at the bear's face, and it didn't nod, or anything cheesy like that, because *it was a bear,* but it did lower its body, lying on its paws, and then it curled up, in the shadow of the cliff, and Aidan lay down next to it so that it was curved around him, protecting him.

Emily and Bob looked at each other again. Even without words, they had nothing to say about that.

CHAPTER 24

EMILY SHOT A look at Aidan: *What now?*

He was being cuddled by a giant, incredibly strong, hungry bear. Which presumably wasn't going to let him go in a hurry.

Aidan nodded very slightly: *Wait.*

Then his face took on an expression of deep concentration. Emily and Bob stood very still, part sheltering behind a tree that clung to the top of the ravine.

A noise: Emily turned and saw a squirrel coming slowly out of the brush to the right. It got closer, walking strangely, occasionally pausing to sniff the air and look around, as if confused.

She and Bob exchanged glances.

The squirrel kept approaching, closer and closer to the bear. And the bear raised its head, muzzle twitching, nose flaring. Its eyes locked, laserlike, on the squirrel.

The squirrel watched the bear. But it didn't run away.

Aidan, Emily realized. *Aidan is controlling the squirrel. A tempting meal for a mother bear to feed to its cub.*

She remembered her parents, how they'd been about to go nuclear on her about the fire, and he'd made them forget. He was doing something similar to the squirrel: canceling its fear of the bear. A frisson of understanding passed through her. She imagined herself as the squirrel: all choice taken away.

And all this time, the squirrel was getting closer, moving in its weird, stop-start, glitchy way, like there was a part of it that knew it shouldn't be doing this, like there was an error in its programming.

Which there was.

Eventually it was too close: the bear pushed Aidan aside with her snout, and rose on her legs, then pounced—but suddenly, the squirrel turned and dashed back, swift as mercury, and the bear leaped after it, rushing, and then crashing into the undergrowth as the squirrel disappeared.

"Quickly," said Aidan, hurrying over to Emily and Bob. They headed downhill, away from the bear, away from the cliff, alongside the ravine.

"Won't she follow?" said Bob.

"I hope not," said Aidan. "Animals are pretty . . . basic. More intelligent than you think they are, as an aside, but still basic. She is distracted by the squirrel. I hope."

"You hope. Great." Bob was casting his eyes nervously up the slope, to where bushes rustled and shook as the bear hunted for the now very fast moving squirrel—or so it seemed.

"*I* hope the squirrel's OK," said Emily.

Aidan smiled at her. "You care about the squirrel?" he asked.

She blinked. "Yes."

"Interesting," he said.

Emily was thinking about something. "Why didn't you just control the bear? Like you did the squirrel?"

"Couldn't," said Aidan. "My self-protection had already kicked in; made the bear think I was her cub. I can't override that. Unless I showed her my true form, and that would have angered her."

"Then the bear . . . if she gets the squirrel—or loses it—won't she follow you anyway?" said Bob. "Your scent?"

"I don't think so," said Aidan. "If we get far enough away, the effect will be broken. It requires a degree of proximity."

"*A degree of proximity*. Out of the mouth of a seven-year-old. Jesus."

Emily thought about this as they followed the ravine down toward the lake, and the cabin.

"Does that mean our—*my*—parents won't think of you as their son anymore? Because we left?"

He nodded. "They will have forgotten me. Every night they forgot me, and I was remade in their memories the next day. At least, I think. Not that we were together for so long, me and your parents."

Oh, thought Emily. This was a weird thought, Aidan coming in and out of her parents' memory, like the sun. In the context of a *lot* of weirdness, but still.

They passed from the avalanche-washed valley into the woods, the low scrub.

When they reached the overhang they had seen from higher up, Emily went over to it and lowered herself as far as she could before dropping to the rocks below. There was no way Bob could do it: he had lost even more color, was breathing audibly, the air rattling in his chest.

She tried not to look at the contorted body of the man in the white snowsuit, instead focusing on picking up the assault rifle lying next to him. She handed it to Bob, who took it by the barrel and hoisted it up. She noticed there was an extra mag strapped to the side with tape. Smart.

He reached a hand down for her too, but she shook her head. She examined the side of the ravine, found the place where it was lowest, and climbed up. A stone came loose at one point, and she slipped from her foothold, eating dirt, but she found purchase again, tendons stretching her skin, and scrambled up to where Bob and Aidan were waiting.

Bob didn't look comfortable with the gun, which surprised Emily: she'd taken him for the frontier maverick type. A hunter. Instead, he handed it to her and she carried it as they slowly descended through the trees.

Now they could hunt.

Now they could defend themselves.

Emily hoped the men were all gone: injured, swept away by snow, dead. She thought that was probably wishful thinking, though. Just because they hadn't seen the third man, the one who'd been knocked down by the exploding gas tank, didn't mean he was dead. He might be out there somewhere, still coming for them.

Hell, even the guy she'd shot in the leg: he could be limping down the mountain, grimly determined to carry out his mission.

The thing they *couldn't* defend themselves against, not for long anyway, was the temperature. It was maybe five degrees, if they were lucky. Emily could feel her hands going stiff and clumsy, could smell ice in the air. They needed to get to the cabin, or they were going to be in real trouble. Fatal trouble.

Also, they needed food. Not as badly as water or warmth, but still. The hungrier they got, the more their concentration would slip, and the higher the chance that they would die.

She could tell they were nearing the lake, because she heard it: heard the creaking, booming, the sound of the ice that remained, water sloshing, deep down under the frozen surface. A noise of cracking, shifting: almost tectonic. They came out from the trees and into a series of gentle rises covered in dense bracken and scrub.

And nettles. If they had a pot and boiling water, they could gather them and cook them—pretty much the only thing worth foraging in the spring in Alaska.

But they didn't have those things.

Emily's stomach was aching with hunger, a sort of dull, constant pain. Bob, she guessed, was feeling worse. He was a big guy, would be used to a certain number of calories a day.

The cabin was still a good distance away; in the clear, cold air it was hard to judge distance accurately. No smoke rose from the chimney, still: it seemed the place was abandoned. This wasn't hunting season, after all. The animals seemed to know it too: as they came down the second of the low mounds, nearing the rocky beach, movement caught Emily's eye and she looked up at the slope above them and saw three wolves, loping away from them through a thin stand of spruce trees.

The wolves traveled long and loose, the lead one—the biggest—

white with gray markings; the other two, darker in shade. They moved over the ground like their bones were connected by springs, not joints—undulating. Living liquid. Then, an instant later, they vanished: gone behind the trees. They didn't reappear.

Emily felt something old and primal prickle through her: a fear, wired into her brain. Stupid, really. They had a gun, and wolves didn't kill people these days. But she caught Bob's eye and she could see he'd noticed them too, because he gave a small nod.

Wolves definitely did hunt other creatures: as they rounded a hillock and came closer to the beach, Emily saw a pile of red rags on the snowy grass that, as they approached, she realized was a young Dall ram, steam still rising from it—a fresh kill, left behind by the wolves.

No: not a kill.

They drew closer, and Emily became aware that what she had thought was warm meat, making vapor, was actually the ram still breathing. Its legs were splayed, its horns dug into the earth. The spine was visible through its back, some of the ribs too, and the skin and hide of one leg was pulled back, like a rolled-down sock, exposing the muscle and nerves beneath.

She felt her gag reflex kick in, and fought it—she needed to do something for the ram, something to help it, but what could she—

She turned, saw that Aidan was moving toward the ram.

"Aidan . . . ," she said, meaning to counsel him against caring. Like her dad had done when she first shot a deer. The way of the natural world, that sort of thing.

But he ignored her.

The little boy got right up close to the sheep, then dropped to one knee. He looked into the animal's visible eye, which was rolling in pain. The ram was foaming at the mouth.

"Horrible thing," said Bob, making an attempt to carry on.

But Aidan was paying no attention to him or to Emily. He crouched and put a hand on the ram's neck; held it there while looking into its eye.

Gradually the animal slowed, calmed, until it was just gazing up at him, and then it let out one long last breath, like a sigh.

The large brown eye closed, and the ram lay still.

For a moment, everything was silent. Even the lake stopped its groaning.

Aidan stood.

"What did you do?" said Emily.

"They have memories," said Aidan. "Just pictures, but still. I took it to its mother. To the meadow where it was born."

Emily didn't know what to say to that.

She stepped forward and took Aidan's hand. She held it tight. He smiled at her.

"Thank you," she said. Embarrassingly, tears pricked at her eyes.

He nodded.

They began to walk away. "We should be taking some of the meat," said Bob.

"I know," said Emily. Part of her wanted to. Her stomach, especially. It was tingling, empty—a space inside her she had never been this aware of before, a vacuum.

"But I don't want to," said Bob.

"Me neither," she said. "It wouldn't feel right."

When they reached the edge of the pebble beach, Bob drew closer to Aidan. "What you were telling us about . . . about memories. Can you do that with people? Take them to . . ." He paused. ". . . places?"

"Yes," said Aidan.

Bob bit his lip.

"Is there somewhere you would like to revisit?" asked Aidan.

"Don't say words like *revisit*. You still look like a kid. It's freaky."

"OK."

"Good."

"But is there?" said Aidan.

Bob pulled at his ear. "I don't know," he said. "Forget I asked."

Just then a pair of ptarmigans clattered and flapped up from the brush ahead of them. Emily's hands raised the rifle without her mind having any say at all, and her finger pulled the trigger: bullets sent tracer trails into the air, pulling up and to the right, just missing Aidan, who was ahead again.

Aidan and Bob turned to her.

"Sorry," she said.

"If those had been men," said Aidan, "I think you would have missed."

The flurry of the ptarmigans' wings had turned to smooth downward strokes, as they came back to earth a safe distance away, pushing the air, softening their landing.

"Yes, thank you," said Emily. "I realize that."

She rolled her eyes, but Bob was looking serious. His eyes took in the mountains around them.

"If there are any men within miles," he said, "they'll have heard those shots."

Damn it. She turned and looked up at the mountains. A shadow, on the tree line, that could have been . . . No. Just a cloud, passing over.

Still. She had an uncomfortable feeling. A feeling like they were being watched.

What if there was a man still out there?

What if there were two?

Emily pressed on but slung the gun behind her back. Her legs felt weak. She glanced at Bob, and he was white as paper.

Not good.

Not good at all.

CHAPTER 25

THEY CAME OUT of the bracken and onto a beach of pebbles and larger stones, a mercy for Emily because the snow was starting to get into her boots. This was easier for walking: but the curve of the lake also meant it would take longer to reach the cabin, which was on its shore.

They were lucky, of course: in winter they would've needed not just boots but several layers of socks, newspaper packed into them too, anything to prevent frostbite and gangrene. As it was, Emily was concerned about the loss of sensation in her toes: they had been sore and throbbing, and now she didn't feel them at all.

The stones did not prove such a mercy for Bob. Their strange little band had rounded the top of the lake, and the cabin was maybe three miles away, when one of the larger stones rolled under his foot and he went down, heavily, on his side. Emily rushed to him.

"Damn it," he said. "That's my ankle."

She crouched by him. He was fortunate that he too had been wearing boots when the plane went down, that his ankles were at least partly protected by the stiff leather: hopefully, it would just be a sprain. She helped him up, his arm over her shoulder. She handed the rifle to Aidan. "Here. Carry this."

Aidan took it and pulled a face. "I wish I could help to carry Bob," he said. "But I'm not . . . physically strong. In any incarnation."

"Don't say words like that," said Bob. "I told you."

"Sorry," said Aidan.

In movies, aliens were always terrifying; powerful. And Aidan *was* powerful: the things he could make you see, the things he could make you remember. But he was vulnerable to the cold—Emily knew that well—and he was no stronger, bodily, than the little boy he appeared to be.

An arctic tern flew low over the lake, its breast picking up a blue tinge from the ice, as if the lake was its own light source.

Bob limped and hopped, and Emily supported his weight, and it felt like it took hours to cover a few hundred yards. In fact, it probably did take hours, because the sun was going down over the mountains, the high snow clouds turning red and orange under a sky the blue of ice, a fire without heat, up there in the heavens.

Emily thought a fire *with* heat would be nice. The cold was deep in her fingers now, her toes—a bone ache—and she was hungry. So hungry.

To keep herself going, she tried to make conversation with Bob, though he was monosyllabic at the best of times.

"If we get out of here . . . ," she said.

"Yeah?"

"Will you get another plane?" she said. "I mean, was it insured?"

"Yep," he said.

They kept going awhile in complete silence.

It was when they were resting by the lake shore, Emily breathing deeply from the exertion of taking his weight as he limped, that he asked her a question. She'd been scanning the mountains behind them, looking for movement, for the silhouette of a man, or men. They were way outside hunting season, so anyone they did see would be after them. No question.

Bob's question was a lot less evident:

"After you've sent his message and beamed him up or whatever, what will you do?" Bob said.

"Me?"

"Yes. You."

She glanced ahead at Aidan, who was skimming stones on the glassy surface of the lake. No one had taught him that, of course. Presumably he had picked it up from someone's memories. Maybe Bob's, or her father's, certainly not hers because she was no good at it—though her mom was an expert, could make a flat stone bounce a dozen times before it sank, so it could have been from her.

"Go home, I guess," she said.

"You don't sound very happy about it."

She shrugged.

She didn't say:

Home is a trap. Home is all those days stretching ahead of me, days of being confined to a school I don't like, in a town so small it's barely on the map, where without Aidan to hypnotize them or whatever everyone is going to call me an arsonist.

She got her arm under Bob again, took his weight again, keeping him moving. Staying too still would mean hypothermia. Would mean death.

Had to keep him going.

What would an adult ask? Emily wondered.

After a time she said, "Do you have a . . . a wife? Kids?"

"Wife," he said. "No kids. But I don't think my wife will be wanting to see me, even if I get out of this alive."

"You sound very sure about that."

He looked away. "Yeah."

"We're probably on the news," Emily said. "She might be worried about you. She must be worried about you."

"She might. But I let her down bad."

"Was it . . . um . . . infidelity?" She said it, and immediately she felt stupid. But the pastor was always talking about infidelity in church. That is, he was always talking, in church, about infidelity. Infidelity actually *in* church would have made Pastor Norcross's bushy eyebrows rise right off his face.

Bob gave a hollow laugh. "No," he said. "Something happened, and I . . . I didn't handle it well. Drank a lot. Flew a lot. Wasn't around a lot." There were tears in his eyes. She could see them glittering in the low light. "Funny how it goes: when you need people the most, you sometimes push them away."

She thought of her parents. Shoved the thought into the recesses of her mind.

"Huh," she said noncommittally.

"Anyway," said Bob. "We can't make the cabin today." He said it flat, like it didn't matter, even though it was bad. Very bad.

She looked ahead. He was right. The cabin was still two miles away, at least, and the sun was nothing but an orange glow over the mountains.

She looked at her watch. A G-Shock. Her parents had given it to her for her last birthday. She'd have preferred the iPhone she'd asked for, but at least the Casio was indestructible and always told the right time, thanks to its radio and GPS connections.

4:16 p.m.

Seeing the watch, something stirred in her mind—some worry: a lake-bottom creature, moving in the silt. Then it was gone.

She nodded to Bob. "We'll have to make a fire here," she said. Said it casually, mimicking his apparent lack of concern, though she was scanning the hillsides at the same time. Watching out for anyone who might be following them, who would see the flames.

"There's nowhere to hide anyway," said Bob, reading her mind. "Not without leaves on the trees. If they're coming, we're screwed, whether we light a fire or not."

"Yeah," she said.

Actually, they were more screwed *without* the fire—they would freeze and die. Especially Aidan. Or Aidan first, more accurately. He would die, and then she and Bob would die, holding on to one another for meager warmth. It wasn't a comforting image.

She looked around for shelter. If there had been a low branch, parallel to the ground, and if they had a tarpaulin, they could have made a simple tent shelter, but there wasn't and they didn't.

They had:

Well, the same as before. A lighter, basically.

No: they had a gun now too. But it wasn't much use for shelter.

Or for eating.

There was no choice. Emily would have to build a fire on the beach, surrounded by stones, entirely visible to the upland around them, and they would have to sleep as close to it as possible, for that all-important warmth.

And hope the men somehow wouldn't see them.

CHAPTER 26

EMILY TURNED TO Aidan. Tried to keep her voice calm. "Can you get kindling? Tinder? Look for dry moss and leaves and stuff?"

"Ten-four," he said. That was definitely a phrase he'd got from her dad.

He gathered fire-starting material while she looked for wood: there were good dry branches at the forest's edge, washed up long ago by some swell on the lake.

Quickly she built a fire, Aidan ferrying her the tinder, which she lit with the lighter before wigwamming small twigs on top of it, and then larger ones, and larger still, until there was a roaring, flaming firepit, surrounded by big beach stones. The sky was getting dark now.

Water was easy at least, this time. The lake was full of it: the unfrozen edges anyway. They each kneeled and drank as much as they could; but not so much that it would hurt their stomachs, which felt painfully hollow—Emily's was a void inside her, a missing space where the concept of food should be. Aidan drank too:

as he said, all living things needed water. She had to help Bob to the water's edge and lower him to it—her back was screaming at her by the time they returned to the fire.

"If I need the toilet, I'm wiping my ass on my own," he said with a scowl.

"Ugh," she said. "No argument from me."

They smiled at each other. Something was still troubling her, though, something scaled, and ancient, sand shifting as it moved, invisible beneath it, in the depths of her mind.

They didn't speak much, any of them. They just huddled by the crackling fire. It sent sparks high into the dark night air, to mingle with the stars, hot red dying ones among the white glowing ones that never went out but only moved slowly across the sky as she lay there looking up.

She held Aidan close, pressed against her.

"Are you warm enough?" she asked.

"No," he said. "But also yes. Thank you."

She knew what he meant.

As the night wore on, she moved away from him only to stoke the fire, to add more fuel to it. Then each time she wrapped him again in her limbs, imagined heat radiating out from her, a red wave she couldn't see, keeping him alive. She had to keep him alive. She had to get him home.

At some point, despite herself, she fell asleep.

At some point after *that,* she woke gasping, the fire spilling buttery light over the pebbles of the beach.

And as she woke, she knew what had bothered her earlier when she'd looked at her watch.

GPS, she thought.

CHAPTER 27

SHE KNEW SHE should wake Bob right away, tell him what she'd realized, deal with it. That was the safest thing to do if they didn't want to get shot, or worse. But Bob's snoring was labored, and his skin was shiny with sweat despite the cold: a little more sleep might mean the difference between life and death.

The difference between life and death. People talked about that as if they knew what it was. What the difference was. Emily didn't. What was the difference between the atoms of a Dall ram when it was alive and when its heart stopped beating?

Maybe Aidan knew.

Emily held Aidan close to her, willing her life force to seep into him, the heat of her body, of her blood.

That first night after she'd found him, Aidan had almost died. There were lots of things he knew, and, it turned out, there were lots he didn't. They'd returned to the woods behind the house to conceal his ship better—sneaking out of the back door when her parents were watching TV. Luckily, the moon was nearly full, so it was easy to see the way. But it was fifteen degrees below. So cold your eyelashes froze if you didn't blink often enough.

She put on her thickest coat, her gloves, her hat. They snuck through the undergrowth as quietly as they could. When they reached the ship, there was the challenge that she couldn't fix its edges, couldn't comprehend its dimensions. Also: it was big, or so it seemed. When she tried to push against it, she felt as though she were pressing on a building.

At first, they hauled broken branches and laid them on the impossible, unimaginable structure. But the branches had slid off, and it was too big. Then Aidan exclaimed, *"There."*

Behind the ship was a steep drop, a kind of fissure in the earth, very deep, lined with foliage and full of old leaves.

"If we can push it in there, no one will see it," he said.

"If," she said. "But the ship seems kind of heavy."

He smiled. He was pale in the moonlight. "Give me a place to stand and a pole long enough, and I will move the earth," he said.

"What?"

"It's Archimedes. Talking about the concept of leverage." He walked round to the other side of the ship. It was weird to hear words like this coming from what looked like a little boy. "We need a big rock," he continued. "And a long, strong branch."

She found the rock easily enough, and was able to drag it—with some small help from him—to the ship. Then they selected a long, relatively fresh branch—one that wasn't dry and brown and wouldn't snap easily.

He stepped back, directed her as she put the branch over the rock and under the ship, then used her weight to push down on the other end, until—inch by inch—the ship started to move.

Leverage: she got it now. It was something she kind of understood, the principle of leverage, from her old dance classes and
from her awful couple of weeks of cheerleading: that something
small—a slender body—could be made to contain springs, to exert
great strength, to loft into the air, to flip, to stand upside down.

They kept having to slide the rock forward and do it again,
and again, until she was sweating and had to take her coat off and
hang it on a tree.

But eventually the ship tipped, and there was a loud groaning
sound, and then it slid into the drop, with a boom and a crunch
and a *whoosh* of leaves puffing up into the air, then slowly settling
down on . . . nothing. A gleam, maybe, as of metal, but just a hole
in the ground full of leaves and broken twigs.

She turned to Aidan just in time to see him teeter, a surprised
look on his face, then fall.

Flat on his back.

Oh, no.

She ran to him and crouched beside him. He was lying on the
snowy ground, his skin not just pale in the moonlight, she realized, but white, drained of color.

"What's wrong?" she said.

"I don't know. My body is shaking. I can't make it stop." She
saw he was right: he was trembling all over. "There is a pain in my
extremities," he said. "My appendages. My ap-pend—" It was as if
he were a robot, winding down, battery running out.

"You're cold," she said, and understood at the same time.
"Don't you have cold where you come from?"

"No," he said. "But I know it from touching you. I . . . I
r-r-remember when you fell through lake ice, and your mom

p-p-pulled you out and r-r-rubbed you all over and p-p-put you by the fire."

She hadn't remembered that, but now she did. The fear in her mom's eyes. The love. It was almost painful to think of.

She touched his warm, fur-lined jacket. "It's obviously not enough," she said. "We'll get you inside, and I'll find you a hat for next time we go out, a scarf, maybe—"

"Oh, it's not real," said Aidan.

"I'm sorry?"

"The jacket. Not really wearing one—I took it from your mind."

That was Aidan: he would quote Archimedes at you but go outside into the Alaskan night, in the snow, without clothes. He was basically naked, out there in freezing cold, where hot coffee would turn to icy mist if you threw it into the air.

After that—immediately after that—she carried him back to the house and snuck him inside and ran him a warm bath, and she wrapped him in every towel she could find, and then she dressed him in her old jeans from the attic, a T-shirt, a thick Bears hoodie.

When they went downstairs, Emily's dad was in the kitchen, drinking a beer. He pulled a confused, amused face.

"Why are you wearing your big sister's clothes, kiddo?" he said.

Emily saw his eyes narrowing.

Saw him shake his head slightly, as if different ideas were fighting in there, banging against his skull.

Shit.

Emily turned to Aidan.

She thought quickly.

"He's . . . getting tall," she said. "Growing out of all his stuff."

Her father's facial muscles relaxed. "Right," he said, nodding. "Yeah."

"Shooting up," said Aidan.

"You're shooting up," said her dad, an echo. Then he stepped over to Aidan, pulled him into a big bear hug, slapping his back in that way men do. "My big boy," he said.

Emily stared at them, at her dad, who had never hugged her, not once since her tenth birthday; and here he was, hugging a ghost, hugging an idea. She couldn't believe it.

Still: Aidan needed clothes to keep him warm, and she didn't have a jacket his size. So not long after that, she broke into her money from babysitting back in Minnesota and went to the general store and bought him the puffy coat he was wearing right now.

Without her, he would have died in that cold.

Without her now, he might still die.

Bob too: his breath as he slept had liquid in it, as if the lake were reaching out and down his nose, into his lungs.

She looked up at the sparks and the stars, dancing around each other, and she didn't sleep again for even one minute.

CHAPTER 28

SHE WAITED TILL sunlight filtered through the clouds before she woke Bob. The fire had died down, and Emily was afraid that if they didn't get moving soon, they might never get moving. But there was the GPS to deal with.

Bob was sleeping fitfully—she watched him twitching by the embers, and when she touched his side to rouse him, she could feel the heat radiating off him. Not good. She shook him gently. He wasn't easy to rouse—and there were more bright red lines on his wrist and hand: infection tracing his lymphatic system.

"What is it?" he said. He sounded beat. Beaten.

The lake whispered beside them, a constant susurrus, talking in low tones about the clarity of water and the hardness of stones. Or something. Emily may have been a little delirious.

"The SPOT tracker," she said. "You still have it?"

He sat up with a pained grunt. He took the small object out of his pocket and handed it to her. "Why?"

"The men," she said. "They'll be following it." It sent a distress signal when you pressed a button, but if you knew its details, you could track it without that. Passive GPS.

"Oh, no," said Aidan. "Sorry. I should have thought of it."

She shook her head. "Not your fault."

Aidan turned, watching the mountains. Looking for the men in black, she knew. *Damn, damn, damn.*

"Get rid of it," said Bob.

She nodded. *They* were tracking it, right now, she was almost certain. They'd have known whose plane she was on—there was only one regular plane into the town—and they'd have the means to check the ID number of Bob's tracker, which was a transmitter as well as a receiver.

For all she knew, that was why they hadn't yet made a move, why she hadn't seen them, since the avalanche and the bear took out the last two. They were just biding their time, watching her on a screen somewhere, a green dot bleeping against a black background.

She took the SPOT a little distance away from the fire. The cold shocked her: the almost weight of it, a charge in the air. She could smell the lake. Ice, and something that spoke of fish, of deep fronded places. She placed the tracker on the largest stone she could find, then picked up another stone and smashed it, again and again, until its circuitry innards spilled onto the beach.

"OK," she said. "Let's go."

Bob struggled to his feet—or rather, he struggled to one foot and then collapsed as soon as he put weight on the other.

He cursed, and she helped him up, then got his arm over her shoulders, so that he could limp along, with her bearing the weight instead of his hurt ankle.

"Not far," said Aidan.

It was both true and not true. Under the pale low sun, the center of the lake almost glowed blue. Moonlight, if moonlight were a solid thing.

Emily was trembling with weakness when they finally reached the short path from the lake to the cabin. A large canoe was pulled up on shore, tied to a stump. Bob leaned against a tree, and she approached the cabin door, praying that it didn't have a lock. She didn't do much praying ordinarily—that was her mom's thing—and she knew this wasn't how it was supposed to work. It was supposed to be for kids who really deserved it, but she was too cold and tired to stop herself.

The cabin was low and compact, made from interlocking logs. The roof was covered in turf, and there was a chimney built out of what looked like the same gray stones as the beach. At the back was a small shed structure: a storage unit of some kind, Emily supposed.

The door had a steel catch. Bob propped himself against the wall of the cabin as Emily lifted it . . . and the door swung inward. It wasn't even locked. Well: who would break in? She entered the cabin. There was a stale but not unpleasant smell. No one had been here in a long time. She smiled to herself.

She looked around in the gloomy light. Most everything was made out of wood, much of it hand-carved and turned and slotted. There was a table; a single bed, raised off the floor, covered in blankets. A couple of chairs. Shelves containing oil lamps, feathers, pebbles, the skull of some kind of bird—things a hunter might collect during a season. The windows were thin plastic sheeting: again, made by hand, Emily could see. Well: how else would they be made? There was no way to drive building supplies or builders, for that matter, up here.

Most important, there was: a stove, with a kettle and pan set on top.

A card sign propped next to the pan said: PLEASE LEAVE THIS PLACE AS YOU FOUND IT. MAY PEACE ALWAYS SURROUND IT.

Amen to that, thought Emily, the echo of her earlier prayer still in her mind.

Bob had come in now too, and Aidan. Emily tried to think. They were in a cabin. They had shelter, which was something. Not enough, though: Aidan's lips were blue, even now that they were inside.

Too cold for him. For his little not-real body.

Shit.

What to do? She and Aidan could continue without Bob. But then they'd be leaving Bob on his own. To die, slowly, of septicemia. There was no way to call for help from here.

But to stay might mean being a sitting target for the men who were after them.

Well. She would have to worry about the men later. She couldn't make any decisions on an empty stomach—and Aidan needed to eat, or seemed to anyway. She didn't know anything about his biology, and didn't want to. She didn't need to take him apart to know he was alive, that he understood the important things.

Fear. Love.

The main thing they needed to do, of course, was light the fire. She eyed it. But if they lit it, then the people following them would see the smoke from the chimney, and know exactly where they were. That had been true on the beach too, she realized, but somehow that had seemed . . . better. They'd been outside, free to move.

Here, in the cabin, they were sitting ducks. Trapped.

Bob saw where she was looking, and not for the first time read her mind. "I figure, if they're still out there, they know where we are anyway," he said. "You may as well light it, warm the kid up."

She glanced at Aidan. He was swaying on his feet, and she caught his hands, helped him to sit on the bed.

"I guess . . . ," she said, to Bob.

"You want to send him home, right?"

She nodded. She didn't. But she did too. "Uh-huh."

"He dies of exposure, you'll be shipping a corpse up to the stars, instead of . . . well . . . whatever he is."

"I *am* still here, you know," said Aidan.

"Besides," said Bob. "None of us can think clearly like this."

Emily smiled, sighed. He was right. She looked out of the wobbly, grimy plastic window. Everything out there looked still.

So.

Fire.

Maybe try to find some food. There had to be some kind of stash in here, right?

And *then:* then they would plan what to do next. And who would do it. She was aware, in the back of her mind, like some dreadful remainder in a division problem, of Bob's shoulder, his arm, his ankle. Warm or not, he wasn't going to be able to move quickly.

Another problem for later.

She concentrated on the stove first. There was a box of

matches set into a crack in the log wall, and a pail full of wood and kindling. She took the kettle and pan and the quirky sign down from the flat iron top and put them all to one side. Then she got a fire going, quickly, and shut the door of the stove, adjusting the air intake as soon as it was burning nicely.

The heat was miraculous, immediate, embracing. Bob sat on one of the chairs, his leg stretched out, and Emily resisted the urge to get right up close to the stove and stay there. You wanted to warm up gradually. She went around the single room, checking the oil levels in the lamps, lighting them.

An orange glow filled the cabin—the square panes of plastic in the windows growing darker all the time. Slowly, Aidan seemed to unstiffen, to ease into himself again, from the sharp and folded thing that had been sitting on the bed. He cricked his neck, and smiled at Emily.

He got up and went over to Bob, then bent down by the pilot's leg and put a hand on it. He closed his eyes. A long moment passed.

"Not broken," he said. "But you need antibiotics. The wound in your arm is infected."

"I know," said Bob.

"We'll stay here until you recover," said Emily. She hadn't known that until she said it, but it seemed to be true. They were a team.

"And then?" said Bob.

"Then we need to keep going."

"To send your message."

"Right."

"From where?"

"The HAARP facility. Or what used to be. It was government property; now it's part of some university."

Bob nodded. "I know it. It was on *The X-Files* or something like that. They send radio beams deep into space."

"Yes," said Aidan.

"But it's . . . I don't know exactly . . . a hundred miles away," said Bob. "No way you can make it—especially not with me."

"We may not make it *without* you," said Emily. "Strength in numbers, et cetera. Anyway, let's get some rest and then we can plan."

Bob didn't say anything to that.

The word *radio* pinged in Emily's mind, lodged there from when Bob had said it. Could they send a signal to . . . truckers or something? CB radio? Get some civilian help? She looked around for one. Nothing. Then she searched the small handcrafted cupboards along the wall. She found:

A bag of flour.

Some dry yeast.

A wash of relief ran through her, liquid and cool, frothy with lightness and air. *Food.* It seemed almost religious, finding it here. Like a miracle. Though, of course, it was just a hunter's cabin; there was nothing supernatural about it.

But it meant survival. It meant living another day—two—three. And every day that they lived was another day to get to the facility, to keep moving.

She kept looking. There were also:

Some pots.

Various woodworking tools.

Binoculars.

A Swiss Army knife with a compass. (*Jackpot,* she thought, slipping it into her pocket.)

A medical kit, containing bandages, alcohol, Band-Aids, scissors, gauze compresses.

She did not find:

Antibiotics.

Then again, she hadn't really expected to. But Bob needed them. She didn't like the way he was looking. He was less pale now that they were inside and the warmth from the stove was spreading, but his breathing was still shallow and labored, and he was grimacing when he thought she wasn't looking.

She leaned the rifle they'd taken from the dead man against the wall by the door, ready in case she needed it. She realized she should have searched the dead guy, seen if he had any more spare ammo, a sidearm, anything else useful she could have taken. But she couldn't have—she just couldn't have. Even so, she was annoyed with herself. Her dad would have done it.

To take her mind off it, she made bread. In the absence of drugs, at least she could get some calories into the pilot. Bread was pretty much the only thing she knew how to make—her dad had this thing about not buying bread, when it was so simple to bake yourself, so he'd taught her when she was young. She sent Aidan out with the kettle to fill it with snow, and set to melting it. Then she got him to fetch some pebbles from the beach while she mixed flour and yeast into the snow water.

She set some of the mixture aside in a ceramic cup and put it on the windowsill: it would draw in more natural yeast from the air, make a starter culture, or the beginnings of one anyway. If they stayed a day or two, she could make a sort of sourdough.

While she waited for the dough to rise, she made an inventory of all the things they had: a kind of balance sheet of survival. Lighter, mostly dry clothes, basic first-aid equipment.

Then she built a simple Dutch oven: the way her mom had shown her one time while camping as her dad had skinned and gutted a moose.

There were two pots, one smaller than the other and with a detachable handle, which suited her just fine.

First, she dropped the pebbles into the larger pot, to make an insulating layer of stone and air. Then she put the smaller pot inside it.

Emily floured the inner pot, so the dough wouldn't stick, and tipped the mix into it. Then she put both lids on and placed the improvised oven on top of the stove. Forty-five minutes would do it, she thought.

"Jeez," said Bob, from his chair. She startled: she'd thought he was dozing. "Is there anything you can't do?"

"Oh, yeah," she said. "What I'm told. Schoolwork. Chores."

"Ha," said Bob. "Well, none of those things will save our lives. But you just might."

Later, they ate warm bread, a little too moist, the crust a little hard, but simply incredible after nearly forty-eight hours of no food. Her stomach was full for the first time in, what, three days? And it felt like heaven, it felt like being complete, like being full in more ways than one.

Then they wrapped themselves in the blankets, and she and Aidan took the floor, spooning, while Bob slept in the bed.

Always, they kept looking out of the windows. Expecting to see movement out there. The cabin being encircled. The men closing in on them.

But it was only stillness, and darkness, and the sound of an owl hooting, somewhere very far away and at the same time, weirdly, close.

CHAPTER 29

WHEN SHE WOKE the next morning, no one was holding a gun to her head, and she took that as a positive.

Her stomach wasn't tingling, either, which was also good. Though she *was* hungry.

She rolled over.

Slowly she got up off the hard floor, every muscle in her body aching. Actually, she didn't know that. There were hundreds of muscles in the body, right? Like, in the tongue and stuff. And none of those were aching.

But a *lot* of them were aching.

She went over and took her starter culture from the windowsill, figured she would make more bread.

"I was thinking . . . maybe . . . pancakes," said Aidan.

"I don't know how to make pancakes," said Emily.

"Oh," said Bob, from the bed. "Something supergirl can't do."

Emily hadn't known he was awake; his eyes were closed. She rolled her eyes, even though he couldn't see. "Ha-ha," she said.

"I know how to make pancakes," said Aidan.

"You do?"

"Yeah."

"How?" She knew the answer even as the question left her mouth.

"Your mom," he said. "She makes them every Sunday. I mean . . . I've never done it. But I know the theory."

"I can make pancakes too," said Bob, sitting up. "I used to—" He blinked. "I can make pancakes," he repeated.

"Awesome," said Emily. "You guys are cooking breakfast for me, then. It's, like, twenty-first-century Swiss Family Robinson."

Aidan held out his hand, and she handed him the ceramic cup, now liquid and frothy with natural yeast. He spooned half of it out, added flour and water, and stirred, making a kind of batter.

"It would be better if we had butter to fry it with," he said, looking at the frying pan. "But—"

"Wait!" said Emily.

She was remembering the shed out back. A smart outdoorsman would dig down into the frozen ground, add some ice from the lake, maybe. Make a cold-storage unit. She pulled her sweater back on.

"You spotted a cow outside?" said Bob drily.

"LOL," said Emily, rolling her eyes again. She went to the door. "I'll be back in a second," she said. "There might be butter."

"Don't get caught," said Bob. "Or shot." His tone started off jokey and then ran out of steam, fell flat. He winced. "Sorry."

"I'll try not to."

She went outside, around the side of the cabin. There was a stand of aspen and elm, a low scrubby hill. No one out there that she could see, no plumes of smoke, no movement. If anyone was coming, they were keeping their distance.

When she opened the door to the small structure, yes: there were blocks of ice deep in the ground, and above them, large pieces of cured meat were hanging. Moose, it looked like. Whole haunches, nearly as big as a small person. And on the shelves above there were jars: preserves. Cranberry, she guessed. Blueberry.

Star prize.

Calorieville.

The number of hours they could survive, could go on for, was rising all the time. She almost smiled. But they were still going to have to move, and pretty soon. They couldn't stay in the cabin forever. The smile faded. She hunted around behind the jars and found a bottle with an amber-colored liquid inside. She sniffed it—vegetable oil.

She took a jar of what she thought was blueberry jam and the bottle of oil and carried them back to the cabin.

"No butter," she said. "But I did find these." She held up the jar and the oil.

"Sweet," said Bob.

Aidan took the oil, and poured some into the pan, which he was heating over the stove. Bob had found a large spoon and held the bowl of pancake batter in one hand. He gave the spoon to Aidan. "Here," he said. "You want a full spoonful, but only one at a time. Wait till it bubbles, and then turn it over."

Aidan nodded. He cast his eyes around. "I don't see a . . . like, a flat slotted spoon with a handle? Emily's mom had a thing. An implement. There was no word for it in her head. She just knew what it looked like."

Emily's mom. The words sounded so strange coming out of his mouth.

"Don't need one," said Bob. "We can toss 'em. I'll show you."

The pancake sizzled.

"Now," said Bob.

"OK . . . ," said Aidan.

Bob put his hands, with Aidan's, on the handle of the pan.

"Right," he said. "Slide the pancake toward the far side of the pan . . . tilt it . . . yeah . . . and then . . . flip."

They snapped the pan up together, and the pancake was in the air, turning, and then it landed on the other side.

"Cool!" said Aidan, exactly as if he really was a seven-year-old boy.

"Nice work, champ," said Bob, punching his shoulder.

The next pancake, Aidan flipped himself. Emily watched it fluff up—the amazing alchemy of cooking. Bob slid them onto a plate when they were done, then poured the contents of the jar into the pan—blueberries, definitely—and heated them through, like a sauce.

Pancakes and blueberries: her parents had always made them on Sunday. It was a family ritual. And now they were having them, in a cabin by a lake, far from civilization—Emily and an aging pilot and an alien in a little boy's body.

Life was weird.

Still, it was a change from hiking with nothing in their bellies, and they sat down to eat in the dim light of the cabin.

"This is good," said Aidan.

"How would you know?" said Emily, with a smile. "You have no frame of reference."

"I have access to a lot of memories," he said. "And anyway, these are better than your mom's."

This *was* true. Emily's mom was not a born cook. Emily noticed his *your* too. *Your mom's.* Like he'd said "Emily's mom" when he'd been talking to Bob. This was still new to her. At home, he had always just said "Mom." With a silent *our.* Mostly because there was a risk they might be overhead.

Stop it, she told herself. *He isn't your brother. There's no point wishing he was.*

But that was what he did—she understood that. He made himself the thing you most wanted to protect. The thing that spoke to your heart.

For the first time she wondered something: did she even see him the same way her parents had? The same way Bob did? It was like colors, and how you could never know for sure that someone else was seeing the same ones. There were photos of Aidan: not from before, obviously, but from the time since he had appeared. Photos her parents had taken, on their phones. And they'd looked at them together, though what was to say that they'd looked at the same boy?

She thought of the bear, playing with its cub.

What did Bob see when he looked at Aidan?

But it was pointless to wonder.

Instead, she looked over at Bob, who was getting a little more color in his cheeks, now that he was eating. A very little. But still.

She felt warmth toward him, a kind of spreading expansive luminosity from the glowing fire and the food in her belly, radiating out.

She was here. Aidan was here. They were alive. And Bob was part of their strange little group too.

"You're good with him," she said to Bob, nodding at Aidan. "The pancake flipping and stuff. You'd have made a good dad."

Aidan tensed, next to her. Why?

And instantly: Bob's face went black. Like, instantly.

"Yeah?" the pilot said. His usual blank expression had turned angry, his eyes narrow. "What would *you* know?" he asked. "You're just a goddamn kid."

Silence.

Aidan stared at Bob.

Emily stared at Bob.

"I . . . ," he began. "I mean . . ."

A cold wind blew out the warm embers inside Emily, and she was in a cabin in the middle of nowhere, with a man and something small she had to protect. "Come on, Aidan," she said. "We'll eat these outside." She took him by the hand, led him to the door.

Bob raised a hand, to stop them, to apologize, maybe, but she ignored him.

CHAPTER 30

OUTSIDE, SHE AND Aidan sat on the log that had been placed there, cut-side up to form a kind of bench overlooking the lake. Emily ate the pancake doused in jam, sweet with sugar, tart with berries, and she didn't think about the taste at all, even though some dim part of her registered that it was good. Only about surviving. Only about fueling herself, to get Aidan to safety.

"You don't need to be afraid of him," said Aidan.

She turned to her little brother, surprised.

"I've touched him," he said. "I've seen inside him."

"Hmm," she said. She was thinking of Brad. Of how he always had people laughing around him, of how he could be charming so much of the time. How violence could lurk inside someone.

Of course, Bob wasn't Brad. For one thing, he wasn't even charming on the outside. He was pretty much always grumpy—maybe this was just a kind of extreme extension of that? And Aidan . . . he wouldn't be wrong, would he? He *couldn't* be. People couldn't hide their true selves from him. Their souls. If there was such a thing. Emily wasn't as convinced on that score as her parents.

But good soul or not, Bob had been weird there.

Movement, fast and flickering, and she looked up, startled.

To her surprise, a camp robber bird fluttered down from the trees behind the cabin, stood on the fork she'd left on the plate, and started pecking at the pancake. It snagged a whole blueberry and carried it back to a branch. Chirruped.

Huh.

Someone had stayed here a lot, she realized. Someone who had eaten out here often—often enough for the camp robber to get used to people. She watched its little fast-twitching eyes, its compact body. Soon it flew down again and took a big piece of pancake. She thought it would probably eat from her hand, if she gave it the chance. She had a hunch it had been hand-fed before.

It was strange, but not in a bad way: the proximity, the tameness, of something wild and alive. Something alien.

She looked up at the sky. Clouds were gathering on the peaks, as if the mountains were breathing. The lake was as still as the surface of the moon.

A cough, from behind them. She turned, and Bob was leaning against the doorframe. He was trying to make it look casual, but she could tell he could hardly stand without support; it was in the set of his muscles. She knew about muscles: she had trained hers to do things they wouldn't naturally do, to carry out poses and make movements that used hidden strength to convey softness, to convey grace.

"I said I have no kids," said Bob, unprompted. "Well . . . I don't have any. But I had one."

She watched him; there were no words inside her, nothing she could say.

"*We* had one," he went on, looking up at the sky. "A boy."

Beside her, Aidan breathed out. He touched Emily's hand.

Emily looked at him. Their eyes met. She knew that he had seen this already, that he knew it.

She turned back to Bob.

She watched his face. It didn't show anything; didn't reveal anything. It was like the middle of the lake: iced over. But his eyes: his eyes were like holes cut into the ice, in winter, to get water from deep below, and she was afraid of what might move down there.

She had to turn away, to look at the lake. At the edges it was all water, clear water, with fish in it no doubt. Was there a fishing line in the cabin? Lures? She bet there was. She could try to catch them a fish.

But she had to turn back, at some point. To look at Bob.

"You had?" she said eventually. She put a light stress on the word *had*.

"Yep," said Bob.

"I'm so sorry," said Emily. "I shouldn't have . . . If I'd known, I would never—"

"No," said Bob. "I'm the one who's sorry. None of that is on you. I shouldn't have snapped like that."

She took a deep breath, smiled. "Forget about it," she said. "It's like it never happened."

Bob looked into her eyes. "Yeah," he said. "Yeah. That's the worst thing of all."

He didn't say anything else.

After a time, he went back into the cabin.

CHAPTER 31

NIGHT WAS ALREADY falling, the short spring day coming to an end, and Emily and Aidan were still sitting outside the cabin. They should be on the move, they should be running away, but it was like they were in dreamland, outside of time.

She was thinking that they should probably go inside, where it was warmer, but the stars were so beautiful: splattered spangling across the sky. She was wrapped in her sweater, but the cold was sneaking in around the edges, and into her lungs.

"I'll get us a blanket," said Aidan. It was like he was reading her mind. He probably was, actually.

She knew she should go in, but right then, with the stars above, she found she couldn't move. "OK," she said.

Aidan went into the cabin and came back out. "I think he's sleeping," he said. "Bob, I mean."

Like there was another *he*. Like there was anyone else with them.

"Good," she said.

Aidan had brought a blanket, which he spread over them

both. He was also holding Goober under his arm, the monkey's head poking out.

Emily frowned. She was remembering the plane, when he'd gone back for it. "You really like that thing, huh?"

Aidan looked at her, puzzled. "Of course. You gave him to me."

A firework bursting in her heart, bright splatter of colors. She'd never have believed it—what you could feel for someone so new. Someone so small.

She scooted over—there wasn't much space on the bench, but he was small, of course, and he sat close to her. They didn't speak for a while. He leaned against her.

She put her arm around him and was taken aback as always by the marblelike temperature, the alabaster feel of him—he was colder than a normal person, but not because he was sick; he always had been. She didn't know if it was part of his nature, if his kind ran colder than people, if their bodies worked in a different way, or if they just came from a warmer planet. Aidan had said it was hard to explain, that not all evolutionary strategies were the same and not all environments were the same and not all life was carbon-based, or something, but he'd lost her.

She didn't really care—what she cared about was keeping him alive. He was the one who really *needed* to stay warm or they would never get anywhere, he would never get home.

"We can't stay out here much longer," she said.

"I know," he said.

Ahead of them, the lake was a dark mirror, reflecting the mountains and the stars; the water so still and clear that if you were spun around, you would find it difficult to know which were the real ones and which were only a trick of the light. Above, the nearly full moon glowed through a ring of cloud, a borehole, bright in the black of the sky.

An owl called from the woods nearby, maybe the same one as the previous night—the sort of lonely sound that made you feel sad but also glad of the person next to you, of the cabin behind you. She looked down at Aidan. He was squeezing Goober tight and looking around, transfixed, his eyes wide, taking in the scene.

She looked too, seeing it through his eyes, seeing it fresh and new, as if she'd never seen it before.

"It's beautiful," said Aidan.

Meaning:

The lake. The mountains. The stars. The snow.

"I know," she said.

"Look, Goober," he said, holding up the stuffed toy. "We will need to remember this, when we're gone." He was being deliberately dramatic, deliberately funny, but she knew he meant it.

The words cut her, but she smiled. *Goober.* She didn't know where the name had come from. Goober, though: she knew where *he* had come from. She'd bought him for Aidan. It was the day after he had arrived, and they were in her room.

"You have a lot of stuffed bears," he'd said, looking at her shelves.

"Oh, yeah," she said. "From my parents, when I was little. I used to love them."

"What are they for?" he said.

She looked at him. "For?"

"Yes."

"They're not for anything. They're just . . . toys. To—I don't know—hold. And you kind of pretend they're alive and look after them. When I was a kid, I had them all in my bed, like it was a big sleepover, and I would have tea parties with them."

He went over and picked up a small teddy. "We have nothing like this," he said. "Our toys are . . . *mechanical*, I think, is the correct word. To teach how things work."

"Like toy cars? Construction sets? We have those too," she'd said.

He looked into the eyes of the teddy. "But these are different," he said. He cocked his head to one side, appraising the bear. "This is a toy to teach love."

She blinked.

She'd never thought of it that way.

"Yeah . . . ," she said. Thinking of how she'd carried one bear, Mr. Ruffles, everywhere with her, until one of his eyes fell out and he was dirty and matted all over. "You're right. I guess."

When he put the teddy back on the shelf, she could see the reluctance in his movements.

"Would you like one of your own?" she'd said.

And an hour later they were in the general store, and he was picking out a monkey: Goober. That was the last of her babysitting money from Minnesota.

Now, by the mostly frozen lake, Aidan held the monkey close to him and watched the mountains. "It's strange to me," he said, "that instead of enjoying this place, you people always want to fight over who owns it."

"Not me," she said.

"No. Not you."

They didn't say anything for a long time. Emily could feel her muscles stiffening. She knew she needed to go inside, check on the fire, keep it burning low all night.

"You still think we can get there—to the antenna place?" she said.

"I think we can," said Aidan. A very faint stress on *we*. There was something unspoken there: *but not Bob.*

"Not if we stay here," she said.

"No."

"So we should see how things stand in the morning. And then keep moving."

"Yes."

Emily looked up at the mountainside where they had come down, the valley and the snow field above. "They will still be after us."

"Yes."

"But we'll get you home."

He smiled at her. "Well," he said. "My other home."

She felt herself welling up. She hugged him. Right now, she was in an amazing place, far from home, and she wasn't alone.

"Do you think they'll ever give up?" she said. "On finding you?"

A fantasy: She and Aidan, exploring. Going to New York. London. Paris. She could dance, or learn to, properly, and he could . . . well, her mom could come along too—her dad as well, she guessed—maybe they could homeschool him and—

"No," he said. "They'll never stop."

"Never?"

"They don't understand me," he said. "And when they don't

understand, it makes them anxious. They will not rest until they have detained me and can examine me. That's what my . . . my mother says."

"I don't understand any of *this*." Emily waved her hand at the snowy peaks of the mountains, the faint ripples on the surface of the lake. "It doesn't bother me that I don't. I don't need to examine it."

"And that's why I like you," said Aidan.

She smiled.

Her breath was freezing in her nostrils—she could feel it. She shivered.

"You need to move," said Aidan. "For warmth."

She turned to the door. "Yes. We should go in."

"Or . . . ," he said. "That thing you were doing, when we first camped? When you put out your leg? Maybe you should do that."

She gave him a look, like, *Seriously?* He was being coy, that was why: he knew exactly what he meant, he'd looked inside her. *That thing you were doing.* He knew very well what she'd given up, what she'd stopped, when they came to Alaska.

"No," she said. "We need sleep. Tomorrow, maybe."

"There is only now," he said. "So dance."

CHAPTER 32

SHE LOOKED OUT at the flat-pebbled shore. To dance, amid such beauty. Yes—why not? After all, tomorrow they might be dead. Tomorrow Aidan might be gone. Bob was sleeping. It wasn't like they could leave now anyway.

"OK," she said. "But then we go in. It's too cold for you out here."

She got up, stretched her thigh muscles, her hamstrings. Touched her toes; caught her ankle and held one leg behind her head, then the other.

After that she walked toward the lake. She walked on her toes, beginning to flex her legs. She trailed one foot: leaned down and into a turn, sweeping her other foot around; then a light leap and her arms went out, and she was spinning.

She closed her eyes, letting her muscles remember. She went into something from her old class in Minnesota: a modern piece, a reinterpretation of *Romeo and Juliet*. The movements all about longing, about holding on to something. She made her back a bow, she made her body an arc, and she threw herself into the dance.

That made it sound easy; it wasn't. Her legs ached, her lungs burned. In one way that maybe neither of them had known, she and her mother were alike, she realized: one of the things she loved about dancing was that it was hard; it was hard, and it hurt, and you had to work and work for only small improvements, incremental, eked out with suffering.

And, in return, the floating; the grace.

She opened her eyes: snow was beginning to fall, the flakes almost suspended in the air. She felt as though she were in a diorama. A snow globe. Her arms swooped, straight, her wrists and fingers extended, as she'd been taught, and she jumped and turned and spun, her feet light over the pebbles, as if gravity might let her go, if she forgot about it.

The ground was cold, the stones were cold, but she put a hand down, came to a stop on her knees. Then put her weight onto that hand; uncoiled herself, twisting, pushing herself up just with that hand, a kind of backflip in slow motion, until her toes just touched the ground—

The idea was that it would look slow, look graceful, look like fluidity and ease and no effort, when the reality was that it hurt, it burned, and you felt like you were going to break, but then—

She landed it, transferring the weight to her feet, and straight into a smoother, quicker backflip, one hand on the ground as a pivot, and then—overcome with the love she'd found in the choreography, not in her heart, though it was in her heart too—she collapsed on her side.

She was breathing hard.

She stretched, feeling the singing of her muscles. The snow

was still falling, lit by the moonlight: as if she were among the stars. The lake gleamed.

Aidan set Goober carefully on the little bench and walked down to the beach, his hand out.

"Show me?" he said.

And so she did: she took his hands and pulled him into a turn. She couldn't do what she'd just done, with him, but she danced a waltz: taking the man's part, leading, so that he could feel the flow and the rhythm. She whirled him around, the two of them dancing together in their enormous snow globe, the mountains framing it all, the lake a mirror for the waning moon.

He laughed; he laughed and kept laughing, and she lifted him so that she could skate his feet along the ground, so that he could really feel the grace of it, the almost weightlessness when you were inside the dance—

And then she looked down and saw that her feet were a little above the ground, and then they were above the stones of the beach, in the air, cushioned by it, and turning, turning, and—

"Are you doing this?" she said, and—

"Yes," he said.

They were flying: not high, but not touching the earth, either; they were in the snow, part of the snow, suspended and whirling and dancing, in blue light. They were energy in movement, no effort at all now, all the ease of the dance without any of the pain— they were drifting, they were flurry; they were eddies in the air made into bodies; they were snowflakes.

She had been holding him up, and now he was holding her up. The snow hanging in the air revealed the depth of the world; how far back it went, in every direction, sparkling with white dots in black space.

This moment.

This:

This was the best thing, in all her life.

Then, slowly, they drifted back down, and landed on the pebbles. Emily held him tight.

"Was that real?" she said.

"As anything," he answered.

She was cold; so was he. That was why he'd stopped, probably. But still she didn't go inside, not just yet. She held him, and she tried to hold the moment too: to capture the night and the view and the smell of pine in her mind and the snow—trying to fix it, so she could return to this moment in the future if she wanted to, this moment out of time. She held her eyes open, unblinking, and drew it all toward her, the water, the sky, the moon, the trees.

She closed her eyes. Already it was murky in her mind— a Polaroid of a Polaroid, the detail lost.

That was the thing: the world was beautiful, but you couldn't take it with you. Maybe that was why some people wanted to own bits of it, to have paper putting it in their names. But that was only a kind of delusion. You just had to stay in it, all the time, in the moment, and you couldn't do that when you were always running away.

She held his hand, and they went inside.

On the way he picked up Goober. His people didn't have toys to teach them love. But maybe they didn't need them.

Or maybe they did.

Maybe that was what she was for.

CHAPTER 33

AS SOON AS the sun rose, they should have been running, they should have been on the move, but Emily found herself strangely reluctant to leave the cabin. They were warm there, they had food, they had a view of the lake and the steep rise behind them, and it would be hard for anyone to sneak up on them. Of course, they'd have to go eventually: Bob needed proper medical treatment.

They had to go that day, actually. Keeping the fire burning when the sky was dark, when the smoke would be visible from far away—it had been far too risky already. To do it again would be madness.

But for now, when Emily got up, there was a stove, flour, jam, and a seat to sit on, and those things pulled at her, like the surface of the earth, like gravity.

Actually, morning was a stretch: it was nearly noon, by her G-Shock.

OK.

OK, they would eat again, take full advantage of the food at the cabin, and then they would move. Take the canoe, maybe, and head farther west. Try to keep out of sight, though that wouldn't be easy with the early spring foliage.

While Bob snored and Aidan slept too—or seemed to sleep; he was lying facing the wall, totally quiet and motionless—she searched the cupboards and drawers. She had had an idea she might find a fishing rod or a line, and she was right: in the far left drawer of the dresser near the door was a set of lures and a rolled-up line. No rod—but she wouldn't need one if she found a good enough stick.

Bob sat up, rubbing his eyes, in what would have been a funny cartoon cliché of tiredness if he hadn't had worryingly dark circles under his eyes. His skin was pale too.

"Hey," he said.

"Hey," she said. "You want pancakes?"

"Always. You making them?" An edge of irony in his voice. But not a sharp edge.

"Nope," she said. "I was going to get Aidan to do it."

They smiled at each other. And that was it: friends again.

Aidan, apparently hearing his name, got up. It was that abrupt: one of the things he had not learned about humans was that people insert hesitancy into their movements—interludes, breaks, pauses. They pantomime waking up, for example, with little stretches and turns of their necks, rubbing their eyes, before actually standing—it was something Emily hadn't really noticed until Aidan revealed it by its absence.

What *he* did was: he sat up, then stood up, and walked over to her, with no parentheses in between the actions.

Just: done.

She held up the fishing line, to show him and Bob.

"I thought we could try the lake after that," she said. "There should be trout. Arctic char."

"Fishing!" said Aidan. "I've never done it."

"You've never done most things."

Aidan took a lure from her and examined it. "Your father's father took him fishing when he was a boy."

"How do you— Oh."

He had touched her father's skin, and absorbed his memories— that was how he knew. She was always forgetting he could do that. It wasn't that she was stupid—at least, she hoped not. It was that it wasn't something people were meant to be able to do.

That he wasn't a person—that was the other obvious thing she kept forgetting.

"Fishing is a thing that fathers like to show their sons," Aidan continued. "I have gathered that from films."

Emily glanced over at Bob, who looked down at his boots, lacing them laboriously, looking down almost aggressively, not meeting her eye. She was sorry for what he'd lost, but she couldn't help feeling on edge when he got that look of pain and anger.

Finally the pilot raised his head. As it turned out, there was no anger: there was a faraway look to him, as if he were in the room but something behind his eyes was in another place, another time. "You don't want to keep moving? To send that signal?" he asked.

"Yes," said Emily. "But we need rest too. And food. The men in black don't seem to be on our tails right now."

"Based on what? Taking a look at the scenery?"

The embarrassing answer was: yes. "I . . . well. I didn't see any movement."

"Wonderful," said Bob. "You didn't see anything, so it must be safe. You remember their white suits, right? Their helicopter? These people are not amateurs. And you shouldn't stay in one place too long."

"Not we?"

A pause.

"Huh?" said Bob.

"You said *you*. Not *we*."

He touched his arm, where the wound was. "I don't think I'll be going much farther."

She must have looked stricken; her alarm must have showed on her face.

"Not dying," said Bob. "I don't think. But I might have to stay here while you carry on. I'll call for help once you're far enough away. That way they can't get to you through me."

"How are you going to call for help? There's no radio."

"I'll think of something."

"No," she said. "You come with us."

He stepped forward, put a hand on her arm, lightly. "Come on," he said. "You know what I'm saying is right. You just don't want to admit it."

For a moment she just stood there, breathing.

Finally, nodded. "Yeah. Maybe. I guess." It was true. She'd known it, in the deepest part of her, in the core beneath the mantle of herself, but hadn't wanted to voice it. They had to leave him here. "But . . . not yet."

Aidan handed back the lure. "Later we'll get going," he said. "First we'll fish."

Emily and Bob turned to him, together, synchronized. Like: *The alien kid is in charge now?* A weird moment of solidarity.

"The men are not coming—not now," said Aidan.

"You know that?"

Aidan looked calmly at Emily. "Yes. At least, I know they're not in the immediate vicinity. Also, protein would be good for you. It sustains for longer than carbohydrate. The body has to break it down into glycogen first."

"Um. Right," she said.

So: they fished. They cut two lengths of line and went out the door, careful to shut it firmly behind them to keep the warmth in the cabin, then walked down the pebble beach to the shore. Emily took one length of line and Bob the other. He limped along the edge of the water a little, and Aidan—she was interested to see—followed him.

She tied one end of the line to a short stick, then a lure to the other end. She cast it into the glass-clear water, as far into the lake as she could manage, and pulled it slowly back toward her. Nothing.

She hugged herself to keep warm; an eye always on the landscape around them, looking out for the men in black. She also watched Bob and Aidan, twenty feet away. Bob was saying something, she couldn't make out what, but Aidan was looking up at the pilot, totally intent on what he was telling him. It made her feel a warm constriction inside; she didn't quite know why. Bob got Aidan to tie on a lure, and they threw it out into the lake together, and Bob showed him how to draw it back in.

She turned back to her own line: threw out the lure and gathered it.

Nothing happened.

Rags of clouds clung to the snowy peaks all around.

Then:

As sudden as a phone call in a silent house, a fish struck. She was pulling the lure back and it was flashing through the water, small and silvery over the stones, when a shadow detached itself from a dark part of the lake's bottom and shot after it. She had an impression of an opening mouth, and then the gleam of the lure winked into invisibility as the fish swallowed it.

She pulled on the line—the fish rolled, hard, sending a small wave up onto the pebbles at her feet. She stepped back, stepped back again, yanking on the line, turning it onto the stick to shorten it and tire the fish, which thrashed violently, turning the water white.

Eventually she pulled it up onto the stones, the water shockingly, stingingly cold against her fingers, and she bent to pick up a large one: she noticed that Bob and Aidan had come to watch as she brought the stone down on the fish's head and stopped it flipping and twisting. A lake trout, maybe eighteen inches. Bright yellow fins; green sides.

Bob straightened, and winced. "Now we've got to get one to match, son," he said to Aidan.

They walked off. She wondered if he knew he had used that word.

They did get one to match: actually, they got two, and she didn't catch another. But three trout were enough to make a good meal.

She wandered over to them when Bob pulled the second fish

from the lake and laid it on a flat rock. Aidan crouched down. The light was low and made the expanse of water beside them seem like something made of metal. Aidan touched the twisting trout, closed his eyes for a moment, then stood.

"Strange," he said.

"What?"

"That thing is more alien to you than I am," he said. "It lived in a different world. This is the first time it has felt weight."

She couldn't tell if he was sad or not.

Bob brought down a rock, and the trout went still.

In the cabin, she let Bob dress the fish. He was exhausted now, face gray, but it was a job he could do sitting down, and he wanted to show Aidan how it was done. The boy sat next to him as he gutted each fish with the Swiss Army knife, drawing out their bright, glistening entrails. Funny how she kept thinking of him as a boy.

One of the fish had a mouse in its stomach. She'd seen that before, on camping trips with her parents. Always amazed her: how did a mouse get in there? Fell into the lake, she supposed: a fatal mistake.

She felt a little like that mouse right now: not in her proper element, despite what Bob had said. Pursued. Perhaps to be caught, and killed, by something hiding in the shadows.

She shook her head, shaking the thought away. Bob gave her a plate with the entrails on it, and she threw them outside; they steamed when they hit the air. The little camp robber flashed down from a tree, lit on the guts, and pecked at them.

She went back inside and heated the pan and fried the fish. Eating them, hot, off the wooden plates from the dresser, reminded her of something she had known as a child—food you caught tasted better. It was sweet, and yet mineral, the flesh of the trout.

"This is good," said Bob. "Thanks."

"You're welcome," said Emily.

"It tastes like stones," said Aidan, marveling. "And salt, and rain."

"Tastes like fish to me," said Bob, but he was smiling.

"This is a world of wonders," said Aidan. He closed his eyes as he ate the fish. "You are so lucky to have all this. I will miss it."

Bob cleared his throat. "Do you . . . do you have to leave?" It was a question that could be understood in more than one way.

"Yes," said Aidan. "I do." Slowly he set his plate down. "I am . . . in the literal sense of the word, alien to this place. It is not good for me to stay too long. I would disrupt the order of things. Everything must be in its place. Order must be preserved."

"Oh," said Bob. "OK."

Aidan stood and went over to him. "You showed me how to fish, so I will give you a gift."

Emily looked up, saw Aidan put a hand on Bob's shoulder.

"You're going to heal him?" she said.

"Oh, no, I can't do that," said Aidan. "At least, not in the way you mean. I am only going to show him something."

"Show me what?" said Bob.

"This," said Aidan.

And then Bob was out of the room: not like he passed out, more like he was just gone. Emily could sense it, like his body was now a shell and there was nothing inside, his consciousness was elsewhere.

Gone.

CHAPTER 34

MINUTES PASSED.

Aidan took his hand away.

Bob came back, through the door of himself, and opened his eyes and looked out. Tears flowed like meltwater from his eyes, like a glacier that has been warmed by the sun, and has become a river.

"Really?" he said.

"Really," said Aidan.

Bob closed his eyes.

"What?" said Emily. "What did you show him?"

"It is impossible to explain," said Aidan. "And now I am tired. We will sleep. Another time, I will show you too."

She smiled at him. "OK," she said.

Bob was smiling too, through his tears. "Thank you," he said to Aidan. "That's the best gift I ever had."

Aidan nodded. "You're welcome. Thank you for helping to get me home."

And with that, he climbed onto the bed and rolled over and closed his eyes.

Wait, thought Emily. *We're not leaving?* Something in her gut told her this was wrong. She was glad Bob had experienced . . . whatever he'd experienced, glad she'd had that moment with Aidan, floating in the snow, but they had to run.

Or Aidan was going to end up on an operating table.

What could she do, though? It was dark and cold out there. In here, the kid was warm. And resting.

Bob tried to help with the cleaning up, but Emily wouldn't let him. "Get some rest," she said. "I'll take care of it."

And she did: she took care of the dishes. But she wasn't sure if she could take care of anything else. Aidan looked so small, curled up there, so fragile. Bob was asleep now too, lying back in a chair. His breathing rattled in his chest. It was pitch-dark outside the windows. No. She wasn't sure she could take care of anything at all; not really.

She kept her eyes open. What was she going to do—really? She had only thought as far as getting Aidan out of town, if she was honest with herself.

She could: go with Aidan to space.

She could: run away to New York, to dance. Maybe go to Juilliard, and learn to do it professionally.

She could: live in the wild with Bob and catch fish for every meal and sleep every night in the cabin, and cook everything with fire, for the rest of her life.

She couldn't: say goodbye to Aidan.

But she couldn't go back, either.

She was trapped.

Story of her life.

She lay there a long time, looking at the whorls in the wood of the ceiling—spirals, galaxies, eyes.

Then the noise outside—and she knew. Sound of footsteps on gravel. The men were coming for them, right now. Aidan's eyes snapped open. They glittered in the half dark.

Her gut feeling had been right. They'd stayed here too long.

CHAPTER 35

OUTSIDE, A TWIG snapped. The camp robber was chittering in alarm. It hadn't done that when she and Bob and Aidan had arrived: it was as if it had concluded they were safe, that they would be at home here.

It had been nice to have *somewhere* to feel at home.

What wasn't nice was the knowledge, in the dark, that the man, or men, had caught up with them. She looked at Aidan.

"Lie still," she whispered. "Don't move."

Then Emily shook Bob's shoulder, and he grunted.

"Someone's here," she said.

Just then there was a crunch outside: a boot on pebbles, perhaps.

As Bob sat up, she pulled on her sweater. It was dark, but that didn't mean much: seemed like it was dark in Alaska except when it was summer. She looked at her G-Shock: 1:00 a.m.

She went over to the door and quietly lifted the assault rifle, thumbing off the safety. She debated opening the door. What if she did and died in a hail of bullets? On the other hand, if she waited, she was letting whoever was outside set the agenda. Her thoughts went sideswipe in her head: *flick, flick, flick*. Options. She could stand behind the door, ambush them—but that wouldn't work if they tossed a smoke bomb or a flash grenade into the place.

In the end, she opened the door in one swift movement and slipped outside, the cold threatening to seize up her lungs.

She couldn't see anyone.

Then: a sound from over by the storage shed. The camp robber flew overhead and landed on the eaves of the cabin, chirruping loudly, head turning wildly from side to side.

Emily held the gun ready to fire and inched around the frame of the cabin, toward the rear. She could hear someone . . . no, at least two people—their clothes rustling as they moved. Securing the perimeter, she figured.

She had only one chance, and that was to take them by surprise.

She took a deep breath, frosty air hurting her lungs, and stepped around the corner, barrel of the rifle in front of her. A man was turning away from the shed, a man in black tactical gear holding a gun, and she looked at him through the sight, aimed for his chest, and started to squeeze the—

"Emily?" came her mother's voice, from beside her.

CHAPTER 36

IT WAS TOO late not to pull the trigger. Emily yanked the gun up and to the left, and a burst of semiautomatic bullets fireworked up into the trees, glowing. The sound was colossal, shocking, a physical presence in the world. The figure in black in front of her dived to the ground and then rolled up onto all fours, tense, and was Emily's father.

She stared at him, her ears ringing.

It wasn't a gun, she realized—the thing he was holding. It was some kind of handheld GPS tracker, a grayscale map showing on it.

He said something then. She didn't hear the speech, but she saw the question mark in his frown and the set of his face.

Emily shook her head, partly a vain and instinctive attempt to clear her ears, partly to say she couldn't hear him. Her mother was standing to her right, dressed in warm outdoor gear, seemingly frozen in shock. Her pretty, lean face and graying hair, her green eyes and Bible-group smile, all of it so out of place, so . . .

domestic. So *familiar,* amid the mountains and the burning helicopter and the death.

Emily lowered the rifle and—always remembering the training she'd received from the man now standing in front of her—flicked the safety catch back on.

As soon as the gun was down, her mom unfroze herself, came over to her, and hugged her; a little stiffly, a little awkwardly. "Oh, Emily," she said.

Surprised—her mother had never been a hugger—Emily tensed, then closed her eyes and relaxed.

"Oh, Emily," said her mom again; the sound coming through to Emily's brain now, but distorted, as if the air were hardening in the Alaskan spring into something thicker, something more like ice. "We knew you'd moved from the crash site, so we hoped, but . . ."

"You were looking for me?" Emily said. Her own voice was strange and deadened, filtered through bone.

"Of course," said her dad. He was breathing deeply, steadying himself—his body no doubt coursing with adrenaline after nearly getting shot. He was wearing a heavy backpack, and he rolled his shoulders and neck, relieving tension.

"And Aidan," said Emily. "Right?"

"Who's Aidan?" said her mother.

A pause.

Interesting, thought Emily eventually.

Awful.

Interesting and awful. But, of course, now she had to cover, explain herself, which was a whole other layer to the weirdness.

" 'The man,' I said," Emily improvised. "The pilot, I mean."

It was not a *good* improvisation, but she was counting on her parents being slightly deafened by the gunfire too.

"Oh, right, yeah," said her dad. "He's with you?"

"Yes," she said. A sudden horrible thought occurred to her: her dad, going after Bob for taking her away on the plane, abetting her, or whatever the police word was. She'd never known him to be violent, but he was trained, after all, had been in battles, lots of battles—he'd been Special Forces, and even now he couldn't talk about some of the missions he'd been on. "He didn't know," she added hurriedly, "that we were on the plane. We . . . stowed away."

"'We'?" said her dad, puzzled.

"Me, I mean."

A pause. "I figured," he said. "The manifest for the flight didn't mention any passengers." Another pause. He looked around— at the cabin, at the woods, at the lake. "You walked here?" he asked. "Last radar position was about fifteen miles that way." He pointed, up where they had come down from.

He was strong, her dad, like someone made partly of metal; someone partly engineered: cables in his forearms; girders in his neck when he turned it. The only weak thing about him was his shot knee, but, of course, that was the part he obsessed about. Always ordering different straps and elastic-bandage things, always trying to be invincible.

Emily noticed, almost for the first time, it seemed, that there was gray in his military-short hair at the sides; fine lines around his mouth.

"Most of the way," said Emily. "We . . . sort of sledged downhill on the plane wing for part of it."

171

"Smart," her dad said. "That's my girl. Where did you get that assault rifle, though?"

Emily glanced down at it. *Think, Emily.* "It was in the cabin," she said.

He raised his eyebrows. "In a gun safe?"

"No."

He shook his head. "Some of these hunters . . . ," he said.

"Let's just be glad she didn't shoot you, Jake," said Emily's mom with a weak smile.

"True," he said. He smiled at Emily. "We'd better work on your aim under pressure," he said, half joking. Then he seemed to hear himself. "I mean, glad you didn't shoot me. But . . . if I had been a bad guy . . . Well. You'd have missed."

He stopped talking, like he could tell he was being weird. Emily felt weird too. The whole situation was weird. She'd been getting away from them—that was the point. Getting Aidan away from the men in black, mainly, of course—but also . . .

Getting away from *them.*

Except . . .

Except a part of her was kind of glad to see them.

A pause, as they all stood there in the light, cold breeze from the lake.

Emily didn't know what to do in this situation, how to be. What would happen when they saw Aidan? Would the memories just come back?

Her mom turned to her eventually.

"But, Emily," she said. "Why did you run away? From home?" Her eyes glittered—the start of tears. "We thought you'd *died,* Ems. We knew you were on the plane, we found that out after they lost radar contact. Can you imagine? We thought you were gone."

"I . . . ," started Emily, but she couldn't go on.

"We can discuss all this later," said Emily's dad, skin taut around his mouth. "Let's just make sure everyone is OK first."

Emily was looking at the tracker in her father's hand. "You . . . followed the plane's black box?"

"Well, Bob Simpson's SPOT tracker," he said. "I got the serial number from the air operator."

Huh. She had been right. But now she thought: Where are the men in black, then? Or white. Why hadn't *they* got here too?

A thought occurred to her: a positive one, for once. What if the others—because there were presumably others, a whole office or section or brigade of them, or whatever the word was— what if they didn't *know* that Emily and Aidan had got away? She had blown up the helicopter: What if it had held the satphone or radio or whatever they were using for communication?

And what if the men—the men from the helicopter—*had* all died? What if that was all of them, the one she'd shot, maybe frozen up there because he hadn't been able to walk . . . the one the avalanche hit . . . the one the bear knocked off the mountain-side . . .

The one flattened by the explosion.

What if they were all dead, and no one had radioed for help, because of the helicopter going *boom*?

If that was true, then the men back at base—if there was a base—might still be assuming that their helicopter-load of special operatives had got the prize. Or they might be looking for them, their signal having gone dead, but not sure where they were.

It was something to hope for.

Emily realized with a jolt that she'd never really thought they would make it to Anchorage, to send the signal, to get Aidan out of here, off this planet. Now a chink of hope shone through the darkness.

"Earth to Emily," said her mother.

"Hmm?" she said.

"You were away in space there," said her dad.

"Oh, sorry," she said. *Away in space.* Where Aidan should be. But instead he was inside the cabin. Sitting in there with Bob. Waiting. She glanced at the door. "You should come inside," she said. "Where it's warm."

For an hour, maybe, she was thinking—and then they would have to move on, because if the men *weren't* all dead, they would surely catch up. How was she going to explain to her parents the need to keep going? To get to the research radio facility? She would have to think of something.

Emily took her parents around to the door and knocked on it first.

"It's OK, Bob," she called out. She had visions of opening the door and being brained by a frying pan or something. That was assuming the man could stand—he wasn't doing well, and that was another thing she needed to work out and handle.

She tried the door, but it wouldn't budge. She remembered there was a wooden beam that could be slotted across it on the inside to lock it.

"Who was it? Out there? I heard gunshots." Bob's voice, from inside.

"My parents," she said.

"What?"

"They tracked the GPS signal."

"I . . . Wow."

"I told you they were outdoorsy," she said.

"No kidding."

Her mom was shivering slightly. Stars dusted the sky above.

"Can you just open the door, Bob?" said Emily. "It's not warm out here."

"Yes, of course. Sorry."

The door swung inward, and Emily went in, followed by her mom and dad.

"Bob," said her dad, nodding to the pilot, who was leaning on the door. His tone was as chilly as the air outside.

"Mr. Perez."

"What happened to the De Havilland? How did you—" began Emily's dad, but the question went uncompleted.

Her little brother was sitting on the bed, in jeans and bare feet; the stove was still glowing. Emily had woken up twice in the night to feed it more wood.

Aidan looked up.

CHAPTER 37

SOMETHING COMPLICATED HAPPENED to Emily's mom's face. A rearrangement. A recalibration. Then she gasped, ran over to Aidan, and went down on her knees, wrapping her arms around him. "Oh, my boy," she said. "Oh, my boy."

Emily's dad took a little longer. He did a strange thing—an almost robotic thing. His head leaned to one side, as if receiving new instructions, like something straight out of a sci-fi movie, and then snapped back upright.

"Aidan," he said, relief in it, and recognition too, and confusion, as if parts of his mind were processing different pieces of information.

As if his brain knew two things at once, and only one of them could be true.

"You're OK!" said Emily's mom, who was still hugging Aidan. "We've been looking for you all the time; we never should have let you out of our sight, we . . ." The rest was inaudible, her face buried in his hair.

"He really OK?" said her dad, looking at Emily.

Emily only nodded, still thrown by the reversal, from outside, when they hadn't even recognized her brother's name. Her dad walked over to him, mussed his hair, smiling.

And, though she was only half willing to admit it to herself, she felt a pang of jealousy. She wanted it all: all their love; all their solicitude. Her dad had never mussed her hair.

"We were so worried, we were so worried," her mom was saying, like a mantra.

"Lucky he had his big sister looking out for him," said her dad. "Like she always has. *Unlucky* that she took him on that plane in the first place. That's something we're going to have to talk about. Something we don't understand."

Emily watched her mother, rocking back and forth with a thing in her arms that she thought was her son—whom she hadn't remembered only minutes before.

Yes, she thought.

Yes, there was quite a lot they didn't understand.

Including, of course, that she was trying to get Aidan to the HAARP facility, and then to his real family. And how on earth was she going to explain that?

CHAPTER 38

EMILY'S DAD HAD many useful things in his backpack—that was his style—but the most important, as far as Emily was concerned, was a bottle of amoxicillin.

While her mom sat next to Aidan on the bed, talking softly to him, her dad took a look at Bob's arm.

"This is a bullet wound," he said.

"Yeah," said Bob.

Emily's dad leaned back. "How did you get a bullet wound?"

Emily cut a glance at Bob.

"A hunter, we think."

"A hunter took a shot at you?"

"We weren't wearing hi-vis jackets," said Bob.

Emily's dad looked out of the window, though there wasn't much to see. "You saw him?"

"No," said Emily. "He must have been far away."

"It's not hunting season," said her dad.

"Doesn't always stop people," said Bob.

"True," said Emily's dad. There was still an edge to his voice.

Like, there would be more questions later, like the trueness of true applied only to the very limited idea of people hunting outside of season, not to the totality of what Bob was saying. He took the bottle of antibiotics from his backpack and handed it to Bob. "Anyway. We need to get you to a hospital, maybe some IV antibiotics, but start by taking this in the meantime," he said. "I'm not a doctor, but you're gonna want a capful three times a day, at least."

Emily's mind was running calculations almost in the background of her thoughts. If her parents went to the hospital with Bob, could she and Aidan get away somehow? Continue on?

"Thanks," said Bob. He was sitting in a chair, his leg propped up on the other chair. Emily's dad had confirmed what she already knew—that the ankle was only sprained—though, of course, it didn't help in terms of getting out of the mountains.

"How did you get here?" said Emily to her dad.

"We drove to a spur road about twenty miles east of here," he said. "Hiked the rest of the way."

A pause. There was a conversation looming, and Emily wasn't happy about it. And there was still the question of how to continue their journey. The men in black weren't going to just give up, after all.

"What about you?" asked her dad.

Yep, now it was here. Not looming anymore but present. The storm broken, the cloud emptying out water on the earth, in torrents, in floods.

"I mean, we know *how* you got here. But why? We got lucky, you know. Marvin from the airfield saw you hanging around Bob's plane, and when we started asking questions in town to try to find you, when the police put out a missing persons alert, Marvin put two and two together." Another pause. "Your mom has been out of her mind with worry."

The longest pause yet.

"Me too, actually," he added. "And when the plane went down . . . when it went off radar . . . we thought you were . . ." He couldn't complete the sentence.

Emily grimaced to herself. Great. Marvin was the type who'd usually put two and two together—and get a night in a holding cell for drunk and disorderly—so it was just her luck he'd been on the ball enough to clock her near the plane.

Her dad took a breath. "So, Emily. *Why?*"

"I . . . ," she began. "I don't know."

"Is it because of school? The . . . fire?"

Interesting. So whatever Aidan had done to their memories had stopped working.

"You can say *arson,* Dad," she said. "You can say *suspension.*"

"Fine. Is it because you got *suspended* from school for *arson*? Because Pastor Norcross thinks that you—"

"It's not any of that," said Emily. "I just . . ." What could she possibly say? The truth was, she had plenty of reasons to run away. The insularity of her town. Her inability to fit in at school, at Bible class on Sunday; her total incapacity to care about the things her parents cared about: bake sales, Friday football, church, hiking, hunting.

Because she'd never wanted to be in Alaska in the first place.

Because she had no friends there. Because Jeremy was over two thousand miles away.

Because there was one coffee shop and three fishing-supply stores.

But she wouldn't have boarded a plane in secret because of any of those things. The *real* truth was something she couldn't say, something impossible.

Only, she realized, perhaps the best way to lie was to form it around a grain of truth.

"There were some men," she said. "They kept . . . following me and Aidan."

Her dad tilted his head. *"What?"*

"I swear, it's true." She was trying to sound like a teenager. She was a teenager, obviously. But she was really trying to *sound* like one. Like an adult's idea of one. Someone with incoherent thoughts, impulsive behavior. "Everywhere we went, they were there. They followed me back from school. Men in suits. I felt like . . . like they were maybe there to take me away."

Her mom had come over, was standing next to her dad. Aidan was asking her a question with his eyes, behind them. Where was she going with this? She had no idea.

"Take you away?"

"I mean . . . ," Emily said. "I tried to burn down the school, right?" This was true. Well, not true. But true as far as her parents were concerned. The layers were getting complicated. "And Aidan's so small, I thought they, I thought you—" *Nice touch, Emily, but don't go too far.* "I mean, I thought *they* were official, you know, that they might worry about my influence on him. I don't know. I got paranoid. Thought maybe . . . they were from social services, come to take me away. I've watched too many TV shows, maybe."

"I've always told you to watch less TV," said her mom.

"Social services doesn't take kids away for lighting a fire in a locker room," said her dad, sticking to the logic of the story.

But that was Emily's secret weapon: she was a teenager, she was antilogic.

"I guess," she said. "I just kind of freaked out. And Aidan too—he didn't like those men. You know they came to our house once?"

Her dad didn't stop frowning, but he let out a long sigh. "They did?"

Her mom shook her head. "Census takers, honey. I was there." She put a hand on Emily's. Her expression was solicitous: worried but relieved too. Like: she'd been hurt by Emily getting on the plane, worried about her getting lost. And she was sad that Emily was so emotional, so confused. But there was a part of her that was pleased it wasn't about rejection; that it was about irrational fear. "You know you can still see the school counselor?" she said. "They told us that. Even though you're suspended. If you want to talk about . . ."

A pause.

". . . about . . . the fire."

Emily winced.

"Everyone wants to help you," said her dad. "Us included, even when you . . . stray from the path." *Even when you sin* were the words in his head, Emily knew, though he was self-aware enough not to say them, and Emily was grateful for that at least. "There's no one who wants to hurt you, no men in suits coming to—"

A bullet thwapped through the plastic window, shattering a little framed picture of Jesus on his cross, hanging on the opposite wall.

The second bullet hit her father in the side, spinning him around.

CHAPTER 39

DAD!

Emily didn't pause to think. As her dad fell and her mom screamed and pulled Aidan to the floor, she threw herself toward the door, picked up the assault rifle they'd taken from the dead man. She went to the window—she was expecting any moment a bullet would tear through her, but it didn't happen—and crouched below the sill. Aidan and Bob and her mom were lying on the floor near the stove.

Her dad was levering himself up into a crawling position, and when she saw that, she let out a long breath.

She could feel and hear rounds hitting the outside of the cabin. Her dad was suddenly beside her—jump-cut quick. Leaning against the wall, avoiding the window. She glanced at his side.

"Flesh wound," he said. "Skimmed me is all."

She nodded.

Another bullet hit the side of the cabin.

"Whoever built this built it good," said her dad. His grammar tended to slip in moments of stress. "You gonna give me that rifle?"

She didn't. She popped her head up and scanned the lakeside, the trees. A flash from the undergrowth fifty yards away, and she ducked as a shot chipped the window frame. Another flash. *Thud.*

But only from that one location, as far as she could see—only one shooter. She swung up the stock of the gun, got the barrel over the sill, and fired right through the plastic toward where she had seen the fire coming from. The noise was enormous, head-filling.

Dum-dum-dum!

Dum-dum-dum!

Two bursts of semiauto fire—not too much. They only had a finite amount of ammunition. There was a break for ten seconds, maybe, and then another round of bullets slammed into the cabin.

"Who the hell is it?" said her dad in a strained whisper.

"Wish I knew," Emily whispered back.

"The hunter who shot Bob Simpson with a long-range full-metal-jacket round, maybe," said her dad. He raised an eyebrow.

"Maybe."

"Or someone *hunting* Bob. Or you." He was looking at her.

She tried not to meet his eyes. He was too good at reading her.

"He shot at us when we were walking in the valley up there." She gestured toward the mountain. "I don't know if we strayed into a secret military area or something." The small kernel of truth in the flesh of the lie.

"So they're shooting civilians now? No."

She was still averting her eyes. Her dad would see her lies in an instant, if he looked into them. She gave a noncommittal shrug.

"Some psycho, maybe," he said, his tone less suspicious, and she realized: Why would he think she knew anything about what was happening? There had been no gunfire for a minute now. Had she hit the guy? Or was he just sneaking up on them?

"I guess," agreed Emily, muscles physically relaxing. Feeling bad—she wasn't big on Bible study, but she didn't like lying, either. Relieved at the same time, though.

"Active shooter, they call them on the news," said her dad needlessly, and Emily realized something else: This was how he dealt with stress. By trying to understand, to analyze.

Thud. Thud. Swish.

More bullets, the last going through the plastic window. Emily raised the gun above the sill, let off another burst of fire in the direction she thought they'd come from.

"We can't stay here," she said.

"Why not? Better than going out there."

"No. What if it's not just one guy? What if they bring grenades? Smoke? What if they burn down the cabin?"

He nodded, getting it right away. "OK. So what's the plan, then?"

"I don't know," she said. "You're the soldier, right?"

He nodded again. "Wait here. Keep laying down covering fire. Small bursts, to preserve ammo."

She raised her eyebrows.

"Yeah, fine," he said. "I deserved that." He crawled across the room and paused by Bob, exchanged a few words with him. Then he went to the cupboards on the other side of the room, started looking through them. He pulled out a jerry can—unscrewed the cap and sniffed. He brought it over to where she still crouched, occasionally putting the barrel of the rifle over the sill and firing in the general direction of the flashes she had seen earlier.

"OK," he said. "Here it is. The plan. You're going to give me the gun. Then you get Bob to that shed out back."

"Cold storage."

"Right. No way he can run, so we're gonna hope they assume we're all gone, don't bother searching too closely. You, your mom, and Ade"—they even had a pet name for him!—"are gonna go out the door and book it to the canoe. I'll cover you. Then I'll follow."

"But you can't cover yourself."

"No. I'll just have to run fast."

It was stupid—you couldn't outrun bullets—but what else were they going to do? She also didn't want to leave Bob—but again, what else could they do? The man could barely walk. The word *again* was in her thoughts a lot. Being shot at, again. People coming for them, again.

People getting hurt, again.

Them wanting to take Aidan, again.

But if they did, she would kill them.

Again.

She handed over the rifle and the spare magazine—she'd used up all the bullets in the clip. Then she scooted over to Bob before she could rethink any of this. "You're going in the cold storage. My dad talked to you, right?"

"Yep," he said.

"Got the antibiotics?"

"Yep," he said again.

No need for further discussion. She got him under the arms and half supported, half carried him to the side door. She turned to her dad and gave him a nod, and he went up on one knee, started firing single shots out of the tattered plastic window. Just like that: Special Forces mode. No unnecessary questions.

But there would be lots of questions later. Emily knew that.

She kicked the door open, and she and Bob went out into the half light, the whole lake valley echoing with gunshots. She pulled and pushed and heaved him toward the shed door, then leaned him against the wall while she opened it. He almost fell inside.

"We'll come back for you," she said. "Or we'll send someone."

"Sure."

"We will!"

He smiled. "I believe you."

"Keep taking the amoxicillin. If they come back here, hide behind the meat."

"Sure."

She rolled her eyes. "Stop that. I hate . . . I hate this. Leaving you behind." Tears, embarrassingly, sprang up in her eyes. Welled up.

"I promise you, it's OK," he said. "I'll get out of here. I have to. I need to see my wife; tell her what Aidan showed me."

"What did he show you?" She should have been fleeing, but she wanted to know.

He shook his head. "No time. You'll have to ask him to show you too."

"OK." She still hesitated. "Thank you. For everything."

He smiled. "No. Thank *you*. I'm an explorer. That's why I

became a pilot. Last frontier, all that shit. Thanks to you, I got to go on the greatest adventure of all. I met an *alien*. And he gave me the best gift in the world. Now go. Keep him safe."

She swallowed. "I will."

Gunfire continued from behind them. No time. No time.

He touched her hand as she turned to go, to hide her tears. "I always wanted to explore," he said. "What do *you* want to do with your life?"

She stared at him. "What?"

Gunshots—*dum dum dum dum*. Her dad was going to run out of ammo, even with the extra magazine.

"I ... don't know."

"Then decide," said Bob. "Once this is all over. Survive—and then decide, and then do it." He pulled her, unexpectedly, into a hug, and she froze and then relaxed, hugging him back. As if he were her dad, or something, though, of course, her dad would never hug her. Then Bob gave her a little push. "Now *go*."

He pushed her out of the door and pulled it shut, and she ran back to the cabin, where her mom and Aidan were waiting. She scooped up Aidan in one movement, threw him over her shoulder in a fireman's carry, and ignored her mom's astonished expression.

"Move," she said, and her mom moved.

CHAPTER 40

THEY RAN TOGETHER, through the dark, under the stars, Emily and her mom, Emily slowed by the weight of Aidan, toward the shore and the canoe. Scent of pine in the air, thunder of gunfire.

A bullet kicked up pebbles at their feet. Then gunfire blazed from the cabin, her dad shooting, high-tempo percussion, shaking the scene, the water of the lake shivering in the dim light. Emily felt another bullet whip past her but then none—it was one guy, she realized, it really was, and her dad was suppressing the fire.

Then: "Goober," said Aidan. "I left Goober."

Actually, he said it once and then he shouted it, so she could half lip-read, half hear it; the gunfire was deafening.

"You're kidding, right?"

"No."

She shook her head. "Sorry. Can't go back. I'll get you something else."

He buried his face in her neck, and she carried on running.

They reached the canoe, and Emily basically threw Aidan into it as her mom toppled over into the bottom, an ungainly somersault, and Emily untied the rope securing it, then seized the end and pushed it into the water; she didn't know where this strength was coming from.

Thud.

A bullet hit the tip of the canoe, spitting fiberglass over clear water, then more fire from the cabin, sustained now, nearly full-auto, and it allowed Emily to wade out, the canoe gliding, and then dive into it. She picked up a paddle, threw one to her mom, and they started paddling.

Only then did Emily realize the catch: even if they could get far enough away, out of range of the man in black's rifle, how was her dad supposed to join them? He was going to get shot if he tried to wade to the canoe in the icy water. At some point, he would have to turn away, lower his gun.

A moment: a moment of pure love for her dad, jolting her like a static shock from a person's hand. She met her mom's eyes and could see she was feeling the same thing, and it was as if bells inside her and her mom were being chimed, simultaneously, making a chord.

Aidan took her hand, held it tight. Her mom held the other one.

Just then, her dad came running out of the cabin; she saw the movement from the corner of her eye, and he pounded down the shore, their canoe moving along it, him chasing them, movements slightly jerky because of his bad knee, pain written across his face. He was zigging and zagging, bullets flying around him—he twisted and fired behind him as he ran, at the man who now appeared from the undergrowth, in his white snowsuit, aiming down his scope and shooting, shooting.

Then—

Boom.

It wasn't a huge explosion, wasn't a movie explosion, but it blew the plastic windows of the cabin out, sent fire balling up into the dark blue, and the man in white—the man in black—ducked instinctively, even though he was too far away for it to burn him. Emily's dad took a fraction of a moment to aim behind as he ran, and shot him; the bullet taking the man in the leg, it looked like, and dropping him to the ground, his own gun firing up into the trees and sky as if it had a murderous mind of its own.

Emily's dad kept pace with them, along the shore, then got a hand on the side of the canoe and lever-jumped sideways into it. He took the paddle from his wife, dropped the gun, and began to stroke, furiously. Emily's mom pulled Emily into a hug, crying and laughing at the same time. It was only after, when Emily sat back, drying her eyes, that she noticed her mom had not drawn Aidan into the hug: as if there was a part of her, deep down inside, that wasn't fooled—that didn't acknowledge him as real.

Emily didn't know whether to be pleased or sad about that.

The pebbled shore slipped by.

She looked back—they were nearly out of range, but anyway, the guy was still lying down, twitching, it looked like. The cabin was burning. She hoped the flames wouldn't reach the cold storage, hoped the ice would hold them back if they did. It was fifteen feet from the cabin. . . . It should be OK . . . she hoped. And Bob could move well enough to get out of the way of the fire, if he needed to.

Aidan squeezed her hand. "Bob is all right," he whispered.

She met his eyes. "You know?"

"I know."

It was true. She saw it behind his clear-water eyes. She didn't know how he knew, but she didn't want to know how he did anything he did. The important thing was that Bob was unhurt.

She saw a flicker of movement in the scrub on the shore—to her surprise, the camp robber was following, flitting from tree to tree, like some protective spirit of the cabin making sure that they got away safely.

"What did you do?" she said to her dad. She gestured at the burning cabin.

"Shoved the tank of gas in the stove and shut the door," he said. "Hoped it wouldn't blow before I was out."

This, thought Emily, was a whole different reality. Alternate dimension. Her dad hadn't let her use a stove until she was ten—until he'd given her proper training, as he put it. He'd given her a knife when she was twelve, said she was responsible enough for it now, had shown her how to use it properly—training and preparation, those were his things. Now here he was, blowing up cabins and hoping for the best.

She was cold, the canoe moving faster than she could walk or even jog; the air breezing past her skin, chilling it, drawing out its heat. Clouds covered the sky, reflecting in the lake so that they were all around them, gray, smoky. Real smoke poured up from the cabin; a dark gray vertical slash.

She looked over at Aidan. He smiled at her, and the world lit up. Above, the old moon was on its way out, cradling the dark circle of the new moon in its arms.

The water below them was so clear you couldn't see it.

As if the pebbles and weeded rocks were under nothing but air.

As if the canoe were levitating.

As if they were flying away.

CHAPTER 41

AT FIRST—AND EMILY was glad of it—there was nothing they could do but concentrate on getting away from the cabin. They paddled along the shore of the upper lake, sticking to the edge, where there was no ice at all. The sun was up now—though low on the horizon—and a few white clouds scudded across the sky. Fog covered the tops of the mountains, as if cutting them off—in the frosty air, they looked like towering headless ghosts.

The cold breeze scoured Emily's face, and she buried it in her sweater, zipped her jacket up tight. Geese flew overhead, not in a V but in a straight line, like an arrow, like dark tracer bullets against the brightness.

"There's the runoff," she said, pointing ahead. "It leads down to the lower lake. I don't know how deep it is, though."

"Worth a try," said her mom.

They paddled to the end of the lake and into the funnel of the short, rocky river. It sloped down sharply, white water foaming.

"Brace yourselves," said Emily's dad.

The canoe rushed downward—Emily fell forward, clung to the side with one hand, pulling Aidan close to her with the other. The bottom of the small craft scraped against stone. The canoe rocked and nearly tipped over when they slammed into the bank—but then they hit deeper water, sluicing over the front of the canoe, and—

—dropped

and cannoned, nose-first, into the lower lake, water spraying up like an explosion, soaking them.

Emily rubbed her eyes, checked that Aidan was still in the canoe, her mom and dad too. Aidan shook his head, like a dog, and his hair flicked more water onto her.

"Hey!" she said.

Aidan laughed—a laugh that had relief in it too.

Her dad nodded at her, then dipped the paddle again. There was more ice on the lower lake, but the runoff had made a kind of track into it, and it looked like they might be able to get around some of the lakeside, at least.

They would need to make a fire. They were wet, and that could be fatal in these temperatures. *You get wet, you die.* Her dad would be thinking the same thing.

"We need to get dry, and soon," he said.

Yup.

Emily watched the blueish ice slip by. They neared the shore, the lake becoming shallower, the pebbles at the bottom so close that, if she wanted, she could reach down with her hand and touch them. But she felt cold enough already.

Soon, though, the lake ran out: into a river, or a stream,

really, that twisted down through bracken and tree-covered foothills. But it was too steep, too narrow and shallow and stone-littered—there was no way the canoe would be able to negotiate it. Emily's dad steered it to the shore, and it bumped gently against the earth.

"We'll have to walk from here," he said.

"Walk where?" said Emily's mother.

"I don't know. Somewhere we can shelter."

They climbed out of the canoe—Emily boosted Aidan up onto the loamy ground; there was no beach here, only earth that crumbled when its edges met the lake. Then she followed: an ungraceful lunge into a kneeling position, a short crawl, and up onto her feet.

Her dad stood for a moment, looking at the canoe. Then: "Grab the stern," he said. He got hold of the bow and dragged it out of the water. Emily and her mom took the stern. He scanned the area.

"There," said Emily, guessing his intention.

A large fir had fallen, perhaps in a storm, its trunk low to the ground, its branches still thick with green needles. If they slid the canoe under the branches, it would be mostly covered.

They hauled it over the grass, pushed it under the tree. Emily was shivering badly—saw her mom trembling too. But they had to conceal their tracks, that was the first priority. Emily's dad took a knife from his backpack and began cutting more branches from nearby trees—he handed them to Emily and her mom, who draped them over the canoe, concealing it as much as possible. If someone followed—the man with the injured leg, perhaps, though that seemed unlikely—they would not find the craft unless they looked for it. Which might buy a little time.

When it was done, Emily was sweating, even in her damp, cold clothes, and that just meant more moisture to freeze when she cooled down.

"Let's go," said her dad. "A couple of miles, no more. Then we'll have to make a fire."

"What about the smoke?" said Emily.

"What about dying of exposure?"

There wasn't really anything to say to that, and Emily smiled, remembering a similar exchange she'd had with Bob—except the roles had been reversed then. Above, far above, a jet on its way to who knew where crossed the sky, the low sun lighting the contrail so that it shone, like a shooting star.

Emily held Aidan's hand as they walked through the snowy woods, heading downhill. Not for any reason that she could discern, just . . . it was easier. And quicker. It was also, by pure coincidence, in the rough direction of the HAARP facility.

"This is . . . complicated," said Aidan quietly.

"Yes," said Emily.

They trekked on for what felt like hours but was probably no more than an hour: the unvaried terrain—tree after tree after tree after tree—covered in white snow that made everything the same, did something strange to the passage of time.

Soon, Emily's shivering got worse, not just little vibrations but her whole body shaking, her teeth chattering in her head, rapping out some mysterious Morse code of their own. She gripped Aidan's hand. If she was this cold, he was in trouble. Could he die, in this human form, from the cold? She thought he could. She realized they were both walking very slowly. Her dad glanced back. Her mom paused.

"Honey, we have to stop," she said. It was unclear if she was addressing Emily or Emily's dad—both, maybe.

Her dad nodded. There was a tree with a low, thick branch, just a little way ahead. He pointed to it. "We'll use that," he said.

While he cut greenery and brought it over, Emily helped her mom to lean long branches against the low one from both sides, using it as a beam to construct a tentlike shelter, with a chimney hole in the middle. They swept the snow out from under, and removed as many large rocks as they could—Emily was good at that, with her small body; ducking underneath and picking up stones, which she threw into the undergrowth.

Aidan wanted to help, but when he tried, he just couldn't find the strength to do it for long. Emily's heart was banging in her chest with anxiety for him as she and her mom wove thinner twigs through the branches, making the shelter wall as thick as they could.

While they did that, Aidan helped her dad with the fire. The two of them gathered dry moss and leaves, twigs, small pieces of wood—well, Emily's dad did most of it; she could see he was really just keeping Aidan moving to prevent hypothermia. Then he took a striking flint from his bag—of course he wouldn't just carry a lighter—and quickly got the tinder smoking, then built up the fire, right in the middle of the shelter.

Emily watched. It was nice—and somehow irritating—not to be in charge of this stuff anymore.

However many times she saw it, she was still amazed how

quickly the fire pulsed into heat, into light, glowing orange against the green of the leaves and pine needles. They all edged as close to it as they could.

"Take off your top layers," said her dad. "Or they'll ice up in the night."

"You think?" said Emily sarcastically.

Her dad acknowledged that with a half smile. "OK, OK," he said. "Always forget you're a quick study."

A pause while he kept looking at her, as if about to say something more.

"You did good, kid," he said eventually. "Getting to that cabin. Getting us away."

She blinked. "Oh. Um. Thanks." She felt a warmth she hadn't expected at this.

Turning away, she pulled off her sweater and helped Aidan with his. They snuggled up close together, as if it were something they had done a million times, as if it were the most natural thing in the world.

Her dad took his phone from his pocket. He tapped on it.

"What are you doing?" said Emily.

"Calling Mountain Rescue. Telling them there's a man—"

"No."

"What do you mean, no?"

"I mean, don't call Mountain Rescue. Don't call anyone."

Her dad was watching her, over the flames.

"OK," he said. "I think it's time we talked. There's something you're not telling us, Em." He put the phone down, though. That was good.

She took a breath. Her heart was booming, a bass drum. The

warm feeling was gone from inside her. But if there was a time, then it was now. They had to get to the HAARP radars or Aidan was lost. And they could never do it as long as her parents believed he was their son.

"The thing is," she said, "I don't think you'll believe me."

Aidan stiffened against her.

"Try us," said her mom. She was doing a half-smile, half-worried thing with her face.

Emily wanted to, she wanted to try. But what if she lost her parents as a result? What if they never spoke to her again?

She took another, deeper breath.

She told herself: *It seems like a bereavement, but it's not. He seems like their son, but he's not. It seems like a loss, like taking something from them, but he was never theirs to begin with.*

None of it made her feel any better.

". . . going to explain," she said. "Which might be a terrible idea. I don't know. But I can't think of an alternative. Just . . . try not to freak out."

CHAPTER 42

"SHOW THEM," SAID Emily, turning to her little brother.

"No," said Aidan.

She opened her mouth; shut it again. "What?"

"I can't show them."

She sighed. "I get it, but, look—I really can't see how else we—"

"No," he said. "I would, if I could. But I *can't*."

"You showed Bob."

"That was easier. He wasn't family. He didn't know me."

Emily watched the firelight dancing on his not-real skin. She was starting to warm up, at last, the feeling spreading glowing tendrils through her limbs. The fire seemed almost to hold back the dense blackness of the night, as well as the cold, to make a circle of safety. "And family is different because . . . ?"

"Because if I show them, they'll remember me. After I'm gone. It . . . it will hurt them too much. Raise too many questions."

"Oh," she said. "But if you don't show them, they'll forget?"

"Yes."

"But I won't?"

Was that sadness on his face?

"You won't," he said.

"Show us what?" said Emily's mom. "And what do you mean, when Aidan is gone?"

So Emily told them.

She told them the truth.

She told them that their son was an alien, and not their son at all.

To her surprise, her dad smiled. He scooted over, opening his backpack and taking out a small blanket. "You've had a shock," he said. "And it's cold, you need to—"

"It's true," said Emily. "He's not your son. And we have to get him home—that's why we're out here, that's why we got on the plane."

"You're . . . But . . . What kind of joke is this, honey?" said Emily's mom.

Her expression was hurt, deeply hurt, and Emily hated this. Hated it.

"It's not a joke," said Aidan. "I am not Aidan. You first met me a month ago."

Emily's mom laughed a hollow laugh. "No. I gave birth to you."

"I was there," said her dad. "I cut the cord."

"No," said Aidan.

There was still that hurt, confused expression on her mom's face—an angry one on her father's. Emily didn't know which was worse.

"What are you two doing?" her dad said. "Is this some kind of game to you?"

"I'm trying to *explain* what we're doing. Why those men are chasing us," Emily said.

"OK, so explain," said her mom. Her voice was as cold as lake ice. As blue and hard and lifeless.

"Aidan has to get back to his . . . his family. So we're going to a radio lab. To send a message into space. The men with the guns— they're trying to stop us. They want Aidan for themselves. To . . . experiment on. I guess."

"Because he's an alien," said her dad flatly.

"Yes."

"How do they know about him?"

"I don't know," said Aidan. "Satellite. Radar. They would have seen my ship crash."

Her dad laughed. "Your ship," he said.

"Yes," said Aidan, expressionless.

"I remember the songs I used to sing to him," said her mom, like she was continuing her own personal conversation. Her voice sounded as if it were coming from farther away than it really was. "I remember the Halloween show you both put on when Ade was four. He made up a poem: 'Pumpkin, pumpkin, pumpkin pie, pumpkin pie with your Halloweeny eye.' I remember when your dad and I were having a big argument when Aidan was little and he said, 'Stop being opposites,' and then that was always what we'd say if we had a disagreement, that we shouldn't be opposites. That we should try to make up."

Emily did not remember these things because they had not happened. With one exception.

"That was me," she said. "Who said the thing about being opposites."

Her dad wasn't laughing anymore. He was looking at her with an intense, sideways expression. "She's right," he said. "That was Emily."

"It . . . was?" said her mom, frowning.

Emily was thinking about something else too: about her mom listing those things. Those memories. Like an incantation, like a protective spell. Like, on some level, she knew the truth. She remembered how it had been her and only her—Emily—whom her mother had hugged when they were safe in the canoe. When she was reaching out, instinctively, without thought, showing her gratitude to be alive.

Not Aidan.

She hadn't reached for Aidan.

"I remember holding his hands when he was learning to walk," said her mother, and now she was crying. Maybe her subconscious knew something, but her conscious mind didn't. "It hurt my back—he always wanted to hold them—he didn't cruise along sofas like you did, Emily—but I did it because I loved him, and, and . . ."

"Look what you've done," said her dad to Emily. "I don't know why you're being so cruel but—"

"Give me your phone," said Emily, suddenly thinking of something.

"What?"

"Just give it to me," she said.

"I thought you didn't want me to use it?"

She held out her hand impatiently.

Her dad handed over his phone. She tapped in his code—he'd change it now, but, hey—and called up the photo stream. "Here," she said, handing it back. "Find me a photo of Aidan—from before, like, a few months ago. Any photo. From when he was small."

"Sure." Her dad scrolled through the photos.

Time passed.

The fire flickered.

Her mom made a whimpering noise.

Her father's frown grew deeper, carved into his face, black-shadowed by the firelight.

"There must be ... I mean ... something has ..."

"There are no photos," said Emily. "Because he didn't exist."

Emily's mom took out her own phone, silently, from her pocket. She looked at it for some time, swiping and swiping, photo after photo.

"I don't have any, either," she said.

"Now," said Emily, "you should probably switch off your phones." She remembered reading something about how your cell could be tracked, even when it wasn't making a call. "There are people who want to get hold of Aidan. Bad people. Government people, I think. That's who was shooting at us."

"This doesn't prove anything," said Emily's mom. "It's all crazy. Someone must have done something to our phones."

Emily looked at them both, and her heart broke for them, despite everything. She got up, and went around the fire to her mom, to ... She wasn't sure what. Give her a hug, or put her arm round her, or something, it didn't matter what because her mom recoiled and Emily stood there awkwardly for a moment, her hand hanging in the air.

She looked over at her dad, for support, but he turned away.

Emily went back to where she had been sitting. She sighed. What was she meant to do here? How did you convince your parents that their son wasn't real?

Then a memory appeared in her mind: that squirrel, walking toward the bear, against its will.

"Aidan," she said.

"Yes?" He was looking at her with infinite sadness in his eyes, and she knew he didn't like this any more than she did.

"Touch my hand," she said.

His fingers closed on hers. Cold.

"Do you see the picture in my mind?" she said. She concentrated on it, on what she wanted him to do.

He nodded. "Yes," he said. Then, after a pause: "Yes. I can do that."

"What?" said Emily's dad.

"This," said Aidan.

He closed his eyes, lowered his head. His skin glowed in the firelight.

"Is something supposed to be—" began Emily's mom, but then she stopped, her mouth open.

CHAPTER 43

OUT OF THE woods, the animals were coming.

Emily and her family—her family, ha-ha!—were in a circle of light, surrounded by darkness. The fire burned hot and bright, and lit the grass and leaves around them, and threw long shadows from their bodies.

And into the half light, where the brightness of the fire ended and the darkness began, the creatures poured, from all directions, reverse-fading into view like a magic trick.

A squirrel.

A pair of mice, twitching their noses.

A deer, its antlers brushing the low branches.

A wolverine, low to the ground, bristling slightly.

A weasel, and then another.

And birds: birds everywhere, on every branch—owls, their eyes huge in the firelight, songbirds, crows, even a seagull that had been passing, maybe.

An eagle, enormous against the darkness.

In the middle, by the fire, Aidan, his head down.

"Thank you," he murmured. "You can go."

Emily knew he probably didn't have to do that, to say it out loud, but it added to the theater of it, and now he looked up and opened his eyes and at the same time the animals and birds melted away, back into the black all around them, until they were alone, huddled by the fire, their little family.

Well. Their fake family.

Emily's mom was blinking at Aidan, her hand opening and closing for no reason; some kind of nerve spasm due to stress.

"But how is . . . ," her mom said. "How did you . . ."

"I can feel their minds," said Aidan. "I can tell them what to do."

Emily's dad was staring at him. "Can you do that to us too?"

"Yes. To some extent. It's harder because you're more . . . conscious. I can't make you do things. But I can . . . plant ideas."

"Have you, ever?"

A glance at Emily. "Yes, but—"

"This is insane." Her dad bit his lip.

"Yes."

"Why do we see you as a boy?" her dad continued.

"Why do we . . . think . . . you're our *son*?" said Emily's mom. It was clear the very words hurt her. Like they were made out of poison gas instead of air.

"It's something I do," said Aidan. "A survival mechanism. I make people see me as theirs. As something to look after. I don't mean to do it. Sorry."

"So . . . you implant memories?" said Emily's dad. "I mean, I don't believe you, just . . ." He trailed off.

"No," said Aidan. "You make the memories yourselves. To reconcile the two irreconcilable things you know: that I am your son, and that I am not your son. I *know* your memories, though—your experiences. I can obtain them by touching you."

"Quit talking like that," said Emily's mom.

"Freaky, isn't it?" said Emily.

Her dad glared at her.

Too soon. "Sorry," she said. "But you *do* know, don't you? On some level? That we're telling the truth."

Her dad looked down at his phone. Then up again. "I searched my texts," he said. "I never mentioned Aidan before a few months ago."

"No," said Emily's mom, but it was a longer word than that, it went on, it turned into a wail. "No, no, no, no, no."

Emily's dad went over to her and put an arm around her. She was rocking back and forth.

"It's OK, Mom," said Emily. "We'll get him home, and then you won't remember; it'll be as if it never happened. As if he never existed."

Her mom shook even more, and Emily realized this was not the most sensitive thing to say. It was weird; grief, she saw, was not confined to the loss of things that were real.

"I've lost my son," said her mom, through sobs, as if reading Emily's mind.

"No, no," said Emily. She moved over to her parents, around the hot fire. Aidan stayed where he was. "No, you never had him. It's OK. It's OK." She regretted the words as soon as they had left her mouth. Because she knew it wasn't OK, none of it was.

"I *feel* like I had him. I remember him. So how is it any different?" said her mom. And then she buried her face in her husband's chest and cried. It seemed to Emily that she might never stop.

"I'm sorry," said Aidan. "I'm so sorry."

No one said anything.

Emily looked at her parents, holding each other, her father's shoulders shaking too, and she had to turn away from the pain. Toward Aidan, sitting on his own, framed by the firelight, cross-legged. So small. So alone.

"If he's . . . an alien . . . what's he doing here?" said her dad. An edge to his voice.

"He's, like, displaced, I guess. Lost. He just needs to get home. Surely you get that?"

Her parents exchanged a look. Her father's father had come from El Salvador in circumstances that were unclear to Emily because they were always discussed in hushed tones. Her mom's family was originally German; her grandparents had come over to escape the war in Europe; that was why her mother's name was spelled with an *e:* Liese, not Lisa.

They looked over at Aidan, and her dad nodded slowly.

After that, no one said anything.

Emily sat on her own. She wanted to hold Aidan; to be held by her parents. But both those things were impossible.

Mostly of their own accord, her hands reached out for a smallish branch, meant for the fire, and she took out the knife from her pocket and began to strip the bark, to scrape and shape the wood. For something to do. For something to occupy herself.

To replace Goober.

She wanted to go to her parents, but she couldn't, she was outside their sadness, locked out from it, because their life was not hers, their memories were not hers. Not only that, but she didn't think her parents were feeling much love for her at that moment. She had just killed their son. As good as. But she couldn't go to Aidan, either, because how would it look to them? Like she was choosing an imposter over them, and it wasn't his fault, it was never his intention.

Emily thought of what her mother had always said, when she mentioned having a brother or sister:

We want to give you everything.

Meaning:

Camping trips. Hunting. A school with a football team and cheerleading and no arts facilities at all.

And *not* meaning:

A place where she could keep learning dance; a city, full of people and potential.

She'd mentioned a ballet performance she'd wanted to go to in New York. Matthew Bourne, *The Nutcracker.*

"Too far," her mom had said.

"And we can't afford it," her dad had added.

Everything, it turned out, had kind of a narrow definition. It was strange, though: right then, sitting on her own, in the dim light at the edge of the fire, Emily would have given . . . well, pretty much everything to go back to the way things had been, before she'd run away.

Everything apart from Aidan, that is.

And wasn't that the rub?

She couldn't go back. She could only go forward—and that

meant losing Aidan, and maybe her parents too, if they never forgave her for it. She'd just have to hope he was right: that they would forget him when he was gone.

For the time being she simply sat, whittling the wood, with the looming shadow of the trees around her, and the licking orange flames of the fire in front of her, and no one to hold at all.

CHAPTER 44

THAT AIDAN WAS not human seemed almost secondary to Emily's parents to the fact that their memories were lying to them—though as the night wore on and then ended with a slowly rising sun, it was as if those memories were losing some of their power.

By the morning, Emily's mother looked a little like herself again—the shock initially had rendered her alien, strange-looking, blank. Now she had regained some of her color, though there were still dark circles under her eyes. She occasionally moved toward Aidan, then flinched. Emily tried to hug her, but she stayed stiff, unresponsive. The pain of that was something physical, in Emily's chest.

Her dad stamped out the last of the embers of their fire.

"So," he said. A flatness in his voice. "What happens now? What were you guys trying to do, before we found you?"

"We were trying to get to HAARP," said Emily. "To send a message."

"I thought that was all conspiracy theory stuff," said her mom. "All the alien communication stories."

"It is," said Aidan. "But the arrays *are* powerful enough to beam electromagnetic signals to space. To send a message."

"A message to whom?" said Emily's mom.

"My . . . family," said Aidan. "My ship was damaged when I landed on Earth. I was unable to activate a distress beacon. If I can send a radio burst, they will know my position."

"How were you planning on getting there?" That was Emily's dad: no need to discuss what kind of message, or how, or anything irrelevant like that. Pure focus on the plan. On action.

"Plane to Anchorage, then . . . hitch a lift, probably."

He sighed deeply at this; he'd always cautioned Emily against hitchhiking. But then he turned to Aidan. "And when you're . . . gone. We won't remember? As far as we're concerned, we'll just have a daughter?"

"Yes," said Aidan.

Just, thought Emily.

"It's weird . . . ," said Emily's mother. Her voice was dreamy; distant. "I think I can almost remember already . . . how you were not there, and then there. It's like . . . like paint is fading. And starting to see the brick underneath."

Another sigh from Emily's dad.

A long pause.

Then:

"OK," he said.

He gestured to her mom, who came over and joined him, and they linked hands—Emily realized they had discussed, sometime when she was asleep, what they were about to do or say.

"You may not be our son," her dad said. "And we may not

understand . . . well, any of this. But we love you. And we can see how much Emily loves you. So we'll help."

"You'll *help* us get there?" said Emily.

"It's, like, a hundred miles away," said her dad. "You didn't think you'd get there alone, did you?"

"Well," she said. "I don't know." She didn't. She hadn't. She'd expected them to disown her, to break down, to lose their minds entirely. Apparently, they were full of surprises. But it was like her mom's beloved fridge magnet: YOU DON'T KNOW YOUR OWN STRENGTH. Evidently, Emily hadn't known her mom's.

"We can't take our car," said her dad. Clearly, he'd had a long night, planning. "They'll have the plates. May even have put a tracker on it. Anyway, we've gone in the wrong direction. So we'll have to keep heading downhill." He unfolded a map that had been in his backpack. "There should be a small town beyond the forest, at the bottom of the mountain. We can get a car there."

"*Get* a car?"

He shrugged. "We'll improvise. What about the spooks?"

Emily had explained during the night how she hadn't been lying, back at the cabin, about the people turning up in town, the men in suits coming for Aidan. The men in black. How they had landed in the helicopter and kept chasing them ever since.

"At least two from the helicopter are dead," she said. "There may only be the one you shot in the leg. Of course, they may send others."

"They probably already have," said Emily's mom. "We should assume they're on our trail. We'll have to move quickly, and keep alert at all times. Jake: you'll navigate. I'll take a sidearm. Emily: you carry the assault rifle."

Emily's mom: occasional yoga enthusiast, gym bunny, keen hiker . . . and straight badass, it turned out.

"OK," said Emily.

"Aidan, just . . ." Her mom trailed off. "Stay safe. OK?" That crack appeared in her voice again; Emily could hear the pain under it, sloshing, bottomless.

"Yes," said Aidan.

"That's what he does, isn't it?" said Emily's dad. *His* voice had an edge to it. Shining. Honed. "Protects himself. Keeps himself safe."

"I guess I deserve that," said Aidan. "Truly, I don't choose to do . . . what I do."

"Uh-huh."

"It's not you who will be hurt, though. In the long run," said Aidan. He turned to Emily. There were tears in his eyes; lots of tears; something had rushed up inside him, and out: like a fire hydrant.

Emily was amazed. She hadn't known he could do that. Hadn't known he could cry.

"What do you mean?" she said.

"You saw me as a I really am," he said. "When you found me. So you're the one who will remember me. When I'm gone."

She looked down at him, her little brother, whom she'd only just met, who would soon be gone.

"And I will remember you," he said.

Silence, for a long moment.

Then, Emily went over to Aidan, and very deliberately took his hand.

"Look at them," said Emily's mom, her face window-rained by tears, tracking on her pale skin. "They've always been a pair."

CHAPTER 45

EMILY KEPT HOLD of Aidan's hand as they walked. They were both cold, and their muscles ached, and always she was turning to check behind them for pursuers.

Well.

She was cold, and *her* muscles ached. So for Aidan it would be worse. For Aidan, it could be fatal. She kept stopping, to hold him to her, try to impart some of her warmth.

"I'm so sorry," she said after the second hour, when they were coming down a snow-covered meadow, a logging track curving below them, toward a place where smoke rose on the horizon. A town, they hoped.

"What for?" said Aidan.

Emily's parents were walking ahead.

She made an expansive gesture. "All of it. I wanted to help, to get you to safety, and I just . . . made this. The crash. Bob. The guns."

"It's not your fault," he said.

"I should have just . . . stayed in the house when you landed," she said. "When I heard your ship crash into the woods. Then I wouldn't have got you lost."

He squeezed her hand. "Emily," he said. "We're still alive. We're still going. Your parents have a map. We're nearly off the mountain now. We're not lost. We've come through that. We're on the other side of lost."

She thought about that. "They're still coming after us, though, aren't they?"

"I imagine so."

"And they'll kill you if they catch us."

"Maybe," he said. "But I don't think so. I think they want to study me. It . . . it has happened before. Not to me. But to one of us."

She held his hand firmly. "Kill you. Study you. Either way, you never get home."

"Yes," he said.

"So we're not going to let that happen," she said.

He squeezed her hand again.

The sun was low as they reached the outskirts of the small town—little more than a timber mill and a road lined with houses. Telegraph poles capped with snow. A crow cawed at them from a tree. Emily's dad told her to stash the assault rifle behind a tree, under some branches. They kept the pistol—Emily's mom tucked it under her shirt.

"What should we do?" said Emily. They were passing the mill and entering the main street. A sign said: COPPER CREEK: POPULATION 2,830. "Ask for help?"

"Too risky," said her dad.

"Aidan could ring a doorbell . . . do his thing."

"Complicated," said Aidan. "They might want to take me in, keep me safe inside. It's hard to predict what people will do."

Animals too, thought Emily, remembering the bear.

Emily's dad looked at them. "We need to look for a Ford pickup. F-250, something like that. Not too new. But anything from about 2008 should be OK."

"But"—she glanced around—"how are we . . . I mean . . . wouldn't that be steal—"

"You *do* want to get to HAARP, right?"

"Right." Emily felt her head spinning, like she was in zero G, like she was in space, where Aidan came from. Her dad had once confiscated her iPod because she was listening to Eminem, and Eminem had curse words. Now he was talking about jacking a car. She smiled, a little. "What if we don't find one?" she asked.

"It's Alaska. We'll find one."

Five minutes later, Emily's mom pointed down a driveway. A white F-350 sat there, on big tires. There was a MAKE AMERICA GREAT AGAIN sticker on the back fender. Another sticker read: I HUNT BUCKS AND ILLEGAL ALIENS.

Another had Calvin on it, peeing on the letters DACA.

Yeah.

Yeah, this truck would do.

No lights on in the house.

Emily's dad walked past a little way, then took off his backpack. He kneeled, searching through it. "Damn," he said.

"What?"

"I need a screwdriver. Flat-head."

Emily felt in her pocket and fished out the knife she'd taken from the cabin. Classic, red with the silver cross embossed on it. She held it out to him. "This work?" she said.

"Perfect."

Emily was beginning to understand that there were doors in the world into other worlds, but not like in stories. That is, you could go through an invisible entrance into a whole other realm of experience—a place laid on the same topography, with the same landmarks, but with a different logic of possibility; a place built on the same bones but with a whole different skin—just by making a choice.

The choice she had made was Aidan.

And once you were in that other world, where houses and mountains and trees superficially looked the same but glistened with the potential for violence, everything moved fast.

The cliché was: a dreamworld. But Emily didn't feel like she was dreaming. Instead, she felt like the mood of the world had changed. Like she'd lived in a polite world, a world that wore a fake smile. And now she lived in one that didn't have time for smiles.

Which is to say: she thought there'd be some kind of moment of transition, some discussion, some hand-wringing before her dad did what he did next. But there was nothing. He just walked past her and down the driveway, fast and purposeful. "Liese, Aidan, wait here," he said. "Emily, with me. Keep a lookout."

Emily followed him, her eyes on the house. The curtains didn't move. The lights stayed off. A man walked past on the other side of the street, with a dog on a lead. But he didn't even look over—Emily's dad was keeping his stance casual, and Emily tried that too; they were just a family visiting friends. Exactly where they were supposed to be.

When the man had gone down a side street, Emily's dad said, "Clear?"

She watched the house.

No movement.

No light.

"Clear," she replied.

He flipped the biggest screwdriver head out of the knife and popped the black plastic housing of the truck's door handle. Then he reached inside and yanked on a lever and the door opened. "In," he said. "Scoot over."

Emily climbed into the driver's seat, then slid over into the passenger seat. The truck smelled of smoke, and McDonald's boxes were strewn on the floor. Her dad swung himself in; shut the door. He used the screwdriver again to prize the plastic covering off the ignition switch. A shiny metal slot was revealed. He slid the screwdriver head into it and turned it, and the engine started.

He shifted from N to R and reversed out of the driveway, spinning the steering wheel so that they came to a halt by Emily's mom and Aidan. "Get in," he said. There was a plastic woman in a hula skirt on the dash, and she danced as they stopped.

A light went on upstairs in the house the truck belonged to.

Shit, Emily thought.

CHAPTER 46

THE BACK DOORS of the truck opened, and her mom and Aidan jumped in, her mom pulling the backpack in behind her.

Someone came out of the house, a big man, with a gray beard. He was wearing slippers and a bathrobe. He took a couple of steps down the driveway, staring at them. He was holding a gun, a revolver.

"Belt up," said Emily's dad. He pulled the lever to D, and the tires squealed as he took off down the street, engine revving hard.

Movement in the rear mirror—the man who owned the truck reaching the road. "Get down," said Emily to her mom and Aidan as she twisted around, looking through the back window. She expected bullets, waited for the back window to explode in a shower of glass shards.

But the man in the bathrobe didn't even raise the gun—he sort of stagger-ran, confused, for a few steps, and then stood there, watching them go. Emily realized: he had only just gone through the invisible door. His heart and mind were still in the old world—he wasn't used to how fast things moved here. He simply didn't know what to do, even armed as he was.

Emily's dad, though: he knew. He knew the rules here, the culture, the language. He knew how to move fast, how to decide quickly.

They cleared a strip of mom-and-pop stores and were out of the town before anyone spoke, doing fifty miles an hour. Then sixty. Then seventy. The road was a good one—hard blacktop. Emily's dad drove in silence for ten minutes, and as soon as they came to a turn, he took it, then the next one.

"Emily," he said. "Check the glovebox. See if there's a satnav in there."

She checked. There was. There was also a bottle of water—she passed it back to her mom, before she turned on the satnav.

"OK. Turn it on. But when it comes up with the options, choose the last one. Whatever the least obvious route is."

"Police?"

"Yeah. They'll put out an APB, but it'll take a while to coordinate. They'll waste time going around to the guy's house first, asking questions. We should have an hour. Maybe more."

Emily did what he said. Then she stuck the satnav to the windshield, using the vacuum tab thing. The route pulsed blue on the screen, the truck a silver arrow, gliding along.

"That was fast," said Aidan.

"Tell me about it," said Emily. She was watching her father's profile, the expression of concentration. "How did you know how to *do* that?"

He shrugged. "You've only known me sixteen years."

"You learn it in the army?"

"I was Special Forces," he said. "I can't really talk about my time in the army." He winked at her.

"Can't or won't," said Emily's mom from the back. It sounded like a line from an old argument, or an old joke with edges to it; a script that they both knew well—both following their parts.

Yeah, Emily thought. She'd known her parents for only a part of their lives. *More doors,* she thought, *to other worlds.* There was the one they'd all gone through, into this place where people shot at you and your dad stole cars. But there were the ones inside her mom and dad too—that opened into their former lives, their other lives, their hidden lives; the lives they had lived before they came here; before they had her; even the parts they were hiding from each other.

Some of those doors, she thought, would never open.

She wasn't sure she wanted them to.

CHAPTER 47

THEY CAME TO a gas station with a bar out back, a motel—neon signs flashed WELCOME and BEER and CABLE TV—and a large parking lot. Emily's dad parked the Ford in a far corner of the lot, and they got out. "Grab the bag too," he said. "We're switching trucks."

Emily's mom was walking down the rows. "Here," she said.

Emily and Aidan went over. Emily's mom was standing next to a dark blue pickup, dented and scratched.

"Why this one?" said Emily.

Her mom indicated the snow on the roof. "It's been here awhile," she said.

Emily's dad did his trick with the screwdriver, and they were in the truck in under a minute, Emily sharing the back with Aidan this time. They pulled out of the lot and got back on the road, and no one followed them or shouted after them.

"Wait," said Emily. "Stop."

There was a pay phone outside a liquor store. There weren't many of them anymore and it was beat up, covered in flyers. She got out and went over to it, and when she opened the door, there was a smell of urine, but she picked up the phone and got a dial tone. She called 911.

"911. What's your emergency?"

"Mountain Rescue, please."

"Connecting you now, ma'am."

Mountain Rescue answered.

"Hi," said Emily. "There's an injured man at Upper Silver Lake. He's in the cold-storage shed behind the cabin there. He . . . had an accident, on the mountain, and he can't move. The cabin is . . . will be . . . burned down. He'll need antibiotics. In fact, send paramedics."

"OK, miss, can I just get your—"

She hung up and went back to the truck.

This one didn't have satnav—it was an older model, and the seats were worn—but there was a map of Alaska in the document pocket behind the driver's seat, and Emily traced their route to Gakona, the nearest town to the HAARP facility. She had only the dimmest idea of what they were going to do there—sending a message to space using state-of-the-art, ex-military, university equipment from a highly secretive research facility was one of those things that sounded easier than it probably would be.

And it didn't sound easy.

"It's basically one road, all the way," she said.

Her dad nodded. He cranked up the heating and turned on the radio. Rihanna came on: "Diamonds."

"Aidan always loved this song," said Emily's mom, as if he weren't with them in the car. "He used to sing along when it came on in the kitchen. Except he couldn't say *d* when he was little. So he sang, 'Shine bright like a miamon.' I always remember that."

"But—"

"I know, I know," said her mom. "It didn't happen. But I remember it."

Emily didn't say anything.

"It doesn't *feel* like we're the lucky ones, is all," said her mother.

Emily's dad turned off the radio.

At the next store and gas station they reached, he stopped and handed cash to Emily's mom. "Best you go in alone," he said. "In case they've put out a missing persons alert for a teenage girl and a little boy."

"You think they'd—"

"Yes. They sent men with guns after the plane. You think they can't issue a police report?"

"True," Emily's mom said. She took the cash.

"Water," he said. "Food. Whatever's fresh, but get some dried stuff too, in case we can't stop for a while. Grab a can of gas as well. Jackets, gloves—we're fine in the car, but we didn't have good enough clothing out there. I wouldn't want to break down and the kids get frostbite."

The word *kids* hung in the air for a moment, like smoke. The plurality of it.

"Or . . . any of us," he said.

Emily's mom sniffed, then took a breath. She opened the door. She headed in, and came out again ten minutes later with some of the gear, which she stashed behind the rear seats. Then she went back for more. She handed out bottles of water and hot dogs once she was in the car again.

Emily ate her hot dog quickly. It was the best thing she'd ever tasted, even with only mustard, because her mom never remembered that she liked ketchup and onions too.

Aidan ate his hot dog more slowly.

"You . . . eat?" said Emily's mom. Tentatively. Sadly. Not turning to look at him.

"It's not the most efficient energy source," he said. "But yes."

He chugged the water much more quickly—the whole bottle. Emily noticed—but her mom didn't seem to—that he was looking tired; pale and weak. She didn't know if it was the chase, the running, the last few days. The cold. Or if he just wasn't made for this world.

She feared: she feared it was the last of those things.

"And you need water?" her mom continued, oblivious.

"Everything that lives needs water," he said.

"And you have a . . . family?" she said.

Emily could see the effort the words were costing her. As if each one were a piece of her, cut away.

"Yes," he said. "Yes, I do."

A pause.

"And you need to get back to them?"

"Everything that lives needs family," he said. He turned to Emily. "Everything that lives needs to be loved."

Emily's dad turned the radio back on and left it on. Nickelback. But no one complained.

CHAPTER 48

THEY DROVE FAST, though always within the speed limit.
When they passed a dirt road with a couple of trucks parked on
it, Emily's dad pulled a U-turn and stopped. He popped off the
license plate from the pickup they were driving and swapped it
with another one. Fast. Efficient.

"Have you thought about a life of crime?" said Emily, when
they were moving again.

"Too dangerous," he said.

"You were in the *army*."

"Exactly," he said. "I've seen people die."

"So have I," said Emily quietly. She was thinking about the
man who had fallen when the bear appeared. The explosion. The
man who had gone down on his face.

Her dad sighed. "Yeah. sorry. This . . . it all sucks."

From her dad, that was like sharing. Like therapy.

"It does," she said.

Nickelback was playing again.

"This music sucks," said Emily's mom. "That's what sucks."

Emily laughed—surprised. Aidan laughed too. It was a shining moment—a bubble. Gleaming. Real family—even if it wasn't real. Just for a moment.

They kept driving.

Maybe an hour later, they arrived at a turning with a signpost that read: HIGH-FREQUENCY ACTIVE AURORAL RESEARCH PROGRAM—NOW A DEPARTMENT OF THE UNIVERSITY OF ALASKA FAIRBANKS.

There was a disused military checkpoint, the windows smeared with dust. The road was clear—a plain, boring road through trees, and then the trees disappeared and it was just high scrubland, dotted with snow. They drove for several miles. Close now. Emily could feel a pain beginning in her chest. A tightness. She wanted to make it, to beat the men in black. But if they made it—and they were nearly there—then that meant Aidan would be gone.

A whole life, without him.

She closed her eyes, and tried not to cry.

"It's OK," said Aidan.

"Easy for you to say," she said. She lowered her voice to a whisper. "You're going home. I'm the one who'll be left here."

He touched her hand. "I'm the one leaving."

She rested her head on his shoulder; it was difficult, it cricked her neck, because he was shorter than she was, but she did it.

Emily could see the lab coming for some time. There was a gray field, a clearly man-made shape, and as they got closer, it resolved itself into a huge artificial forest made of crosses taller than houses—linked together with cables. A snow-peaked mountain rose behind it.

"The antenna array," said Aidan as they drove past it. This

wasn't a quick process: the field was vast, with dozens of these enormous poles. But eventually they reached a turning, a T-junction, and to the left was a low white-domed building at the end of a gravel drive. No one seemed to be following them or investigating their arrival.

A sign at the turning said: IONOSPHERIC RESEARCH FACILITY.

Emily's dad pulled up. "There're all kinds of conspiracy theories about this place," he said. "Like, they're controlling the weather; like, they made Hurricane Katrina here."

"They are doing what they say they are doing," said Aidan. "Researching the composition and behavior of the ionosphere by perturbing it with high-frequency radio waves and measuring the results. Isn't that extraordinary enough?"

"It's extraordinary, sure," said Emily's dad. "But people don't understand it. So they make up stories instead. I guess."

Aidan nodded. "Stories are powerful things. People look for them, even when they don't exist."

Silence. Emily's mom sniffled.

The comment hung in the air.

"Sorry," said Aidan. "For my purposes, what is important is that they are able to send radio waves past the ionosphere. They have used them to measure meteor paths. I will use them to contact my . . . my people."

Emily's mom looked at the facility. "But how are you going to get in? You're just going to knock on the door?"

"Yes," he said.

"Well, OK," said Emily's dad.

"You're not going in there on your own," said Emily. "I'm coming with you."

Aidan shook his head. "No," he said. There was no hesitation in his voice, no crack for doubt to get in. "It's better if I go alone."

She looked at him. He looked back into her eyes.

He smiled—and held her hand. "Trust me."

Eventually she nodded.

"OK," she said.

They drove up to the white building, and Aidan opened his door, letting in a waft of cold air. If it were a movie, there would be a big swelling soundtrack, but instead, he just walked up to the facility, rang the doorbell—no need to knock, after all—and soon the door opened and someone spoke to him briefly, then let him in.

The door closed behind him.

CHAPTER 49

"OH," SAID EMILY.

"What?" said her mom.

"I just thought . . . you know . . . something more might happen. Something bigger."

"It still might," said her mom. She was watching the road behind them in the rearview mirror. Nothing coming. Yet.

"What do you think he told them?" said Emily. "Whoever opened the door."

"No idea," said her mom. "Won't people see whatever he needs them to see anyway?" There was an edge of bitterness to her voice.

"I suppose so," said Emily. She reached forward and touched her mom's hand. Her mom gripped her fingers, her dad watching them silently. Her grip was strong.

They sat there without speaking for a while, the engine running for warmth. There was a low hum under everything, coming from the antenna array.

"What happens now?" Emily said.

"Now we wait," her dad replied.

The sun was getting low—the air was frosty, and the antennas cast long shadows, long dark crosses, ground versions of themselves, slicing the earth. They kept the engine running—stale toasted air blasting through the vents. Emily watched the sky. A couple of thin clouds, altostratus, stretched across the blue. The light was strange: there was almost a sheen to the sky, as if reflecting some unseen glow. She wondered if Aidan had sent the message; if she'd see the ship when it came, or if it would be cloaked in some way.

There was a rumble, a vibration—but it wasn't the ship. It was coming from ground level. Her mom had taken out the pistol, Emily noticed. Her dad got out of the car, and Emily and her mom followed. As the sound grew louder, Emily turned to see a black jeep coming down the long road, past the antenna array.

The jeep got closer, kicking up dust, but the disturbance in the sky remained the same—the heavens catching the light strangely, as if concrete after rain, glistening under streetlamps. Something imminent, about to be revealed—but for the moment staying hidden.

A thrum was running through Emily, her whole being buzzing, from multiple sources: the car's tires, translated through the ground; the heavy electric singing of the antennas; and something else perhaps, something she couldn't see.

The jeep was coming up fast now, and then it did a sliding, turning stop just like in a movie, spraying a wake of gravel, close enough for it to sting Emily's skin. She stepped back, wincing.

The doors were flung open, and two men jumped out, guns swinging up as they moved toward Emily and her parents. They were really dressed in black this time. Emily's parents moved to stand in front of them.

"Keep back," said Emily's dad.

The men were wearing helmets with masks that covered their noses and mouths; only their eyes were visible. Professional eyes. Ruthless eyes. "Where's the boy?" said one of them. His voice was tinny, amplified. His rifle was trained on Emily. The other man was aiming at her parents. "No sudden movements."

"What boy?" said Emily.

The man barely glanced at her. "We know he's here. Hands behind your heads."

Emily's dad said something under his breath, something urgent, and her mom, very deliberately, very slowly, held the pistol out, flat, to show the men. Then she bent her knees and lowered, placing it carefully on the ground. She straightened up again, and she and Emily's dad raised their hands in surrender.

Oh, great, Emily thought. *So they've given up.*

One of the men pressed a button on a small device clipped to his jacket. "We got them," he said. "No sign of the boy."

But he was in there; he was in there, and he would have to come out.

Emily lowered her head. It was over.

CHAPTER 50

THEY CAME LEVEL with her parents, and one of them kicked the pistol on the ground—it slid away, spinning, into the brown grass beside the road. One of them kept covering her parents, sighting down his rifle at them, while the other held his eyes on Emily.

"I'm going to ask you again. Where is the boy?"

There was a creaking sound behind them, and Emily turned to see the door of the facility open. And there he was.

A tiny boy framed in the huge doorway. Light behind him, from inside.

The air crackled with a sense of something on the edge of happening, something about to be revealed—like an amp with an electric guitar plugged into it, humming, just waiting for a note to be played.

"Aidan!" Emily shouted. He ran to her, and she threw her arms around him, felt him squeeze her back.

A voice behind her shouted, "Step away from the boy," but she ignored it, held him close.

"Are they coming?" she whispered into his ear.

Aidan glanced over her shoulder up at the trembling sky, then whispered, "I hope so."

Emily pulled away from him and looked at the approaching men. They were moving slowly forward, and one of them was taking out a pair of handcuffs. The other was holding a black baton with wires coming out of it. A taser of some kind?

"You need to step away from the boy *now*," said the man with the handcuffs. Low sun gleamed on his rifle barrel, hurting her eyes.

Strange, she thought. She *didn't* fear them. It had never really occurred to her to fear them. She didn't want to die—of course not—but these men with their guns were not what she was afraid of.

What she was afraid of, she realized, was the thought of a whole long future without Aidan, stretching ahead of her.

"If you want him, you'll have to get past my dead body," she said, and she stood in front of Aidan, her arms out, shielding him.

For a moment nothing and no one moved.

"Kid, step away from the—" began the man nearest Emily.

But then her mom flung her hand out, and he cursed, stumbling back, raising his hand to his eyes, and Emily realized she had thrown gravel in his face, which she must have picked up when she laid her pistol on the ground, and now, as well as being blinded, he had hit himself with the heavy metal cuffs in his hand.

Simultaneously, Emily's dad stepped forward to the other man. His strength and speed were impressive, the old knee injury forgotten:

sidestep

hand on the rifle pushing it out of the way

other hand striking the guy's face

grabbing the gun and somehow twisting it over and then smacking that into the guy's face too.

Except that in fact it went like:

Sidestephandontherifllepushingitoutofthewayotherhand-strikingtheguysfacegrabbingthegunandsomehowtwistingit-overandthensmackingthatintotheguysfacetoo.

Because it was so fast.

Five seconds, and Emily's dad was pointing the rifle at the men, stepping back to cover them both. It did not waver in his hands. Emily felt a surge, tidelike, of pride for her parents.

"Gun down *now,*" Emily's dad said in a voice she had never heard before, a voice that wasn't loud so much as violent, pointedly violent—the aural equivalent of a knife. "I was Delta Force. So help me, I will put you down, and I will not hesitate."

CHAPTER 51

THE MAN IN black with the dust and gravel in his eyes dropped his rifle. It landed with a clatter on the ground. He was still blinking. The other man was bleeding, a lot. Blood soaked his mask. He was teetering on his feet but managing to stay upright.

"You," said Emily's dad. "Handcuff yourself to your friend. Take too long and I shoot."

The man with the cuffs went over to the other and clicked a metal ring onto his wrist, then its partner onto the other man.

"Emily, grab the rifle," said her dad.

She moved as if her body belonged to someone else and she was just borrowing it. She picked up the rifle from the ground and took it over to where her dad was standing.

"What's the plan now?" she said under her breath.

"I didn't think much beyond this."

"You don't know what you're doing," said the man Emily had taken the gun from. His voice was thick, nasal, choking— Emily thought his nose was probably broken. "That thing is not your son."

"We know that," said Emily's mom. "You're still not having him."

"He's not a *he*. And he's a security threat to this country and the property of the United States government."

"No," said Emily. "He doesn't belong to anyone."

Except me, she thought. *For now. Or perhaps I belong to him.*

"A prisoner, then. He entered U.S. air space. He's an invader, an interloper, a—"

"Living thing," said Emily. "And he's going home."

The man stared at her. His eyes were hard; flat. They didn't go anywhere, open onto anything. Just darkness. "What are you talking about?" he said.

And that's when Aidan whispered:

"They're here."

She looked up. But there was nothing. She felt it before she could see it: a sort of tightening in her skin, as if a storm were coming. She could smell ozone in the air. And was that a shimmer, a fish-scale flicker, in the sky above them? As if light were falling on something just behind the air.

And then she saw it.

Above, something beyond comprehension hovered in the vibrating air.

"I'm talking about that," she said to the man with the broken nose.

CHAPTER 52

SOMETHING WAS FLOATING in the sky. *Something* is not a specific word. But it was not a specific thing. It seemed irreducible to a single, simple shape. Its edges and corners were not where edges and corners should be. It was large, and dark, and broadly circular. But it was hard to tell exactly how big it was because it didn't seem to reflect and absorb light in an ordinary way; it was as if there were parts of it you couldn't see, and Emily didn't know how that was possible.

Clouds boiled around it.

A bird, flying past—a crow—fell from the sky, dead.

A beam of light wasn't there, and then it was there, with no in-between state: a perfect cylinder of brightness, arc-lamp bright, throwing black shadows long behind Emily and her mom and dad and Aidan and the two men, who threw up their hands, photo-flash blinded, except that this didn't end, the light from the column went on warping their sight.

"He's not from here," said one of the men. "It's not natural. We need to take him in, find out what—"

"None of us are from here," said Emily. "Not really. We've all come from somewhere. We've all traveled."

Around them, the antennas and the domelike building disappeared, the road too, the black car, their own stolen pickup, so that there was just them, just these human figures and one not so human, standing in a white glow, and all sound stopped, the hum of the transmitters, the engine noise, voices.

All gone.

Aidan took Emily's hand, squeezed it.

"Goodbye, Mom," he said. "Goodbye, Dad."

Neither of them was able to speak, but they nodded.

The world went away, into light, into exposure glare.

"Time to go," Aidan said, turning to Emily.

She nodded. Tears were on her skin. She didn't trust herself to talk. She didn't know what to say.

And then she did:

"I'll miss you," she said. It was all she could manage. It was all that mattered. It was all.

After a moment, she reached into her pocket and took out a small object. She'd carved it the night before, in the woods, when her parents had learned the truth. By the firelight, not sleeping.

She handed the carving to Aidan.

"Here," she said. It was a girl, fairly crude, though she was proud of how she'd done the hair. She'd spent a lot of time whittling with small knives on hunting and camping trips when she was younger.

"Is it . . . you?" said Aidan.

"You mean you can't tell? I'm offended."

"No, no, I—"

"I'm kidding," she said, and squeezed his hand. Some things really didn't translate, no matter how smart the other species was.

"Oh," he said. "Oh, yes, very funny."

"Yes, it's me," she said. "Because you lost Goober. And so that you don't forget me."

He looked up at her, serious now. "I will never forget you," he said.

A pause.

"Don't go," said Emily. "Don't go, don't go. You're family. I mean, I know you're not, not really, but you *are*. Don't leave me."

She sensed her parents, somewhere in the blinding light, thought she heard her mom gasp.

He smiled. "Do you know," he said, "I have seen every film you have seen. All the TV. I remember everything you remember. I get it all from inside your head. It is part of how I survive."

"Yes," she said. The thought was terrifying—all the lies she'd told, all the petty jealousies she'd felt. But oddly reassuring too. Oddly freeing.

"I know everything your parents know too," he said. "I have looked in their heads as I have looked in yours. And, Emily, here is the thing. It is funny to me that you have so many stories about us invading. About us taking over the world. As if war were a universal language, as if it were the thing that makes all creatures the same."

She nodded. She couldn't speak. Her voice would crack. Her

voice would break. Her voice would fall, like their plane, and be in pieces, all over the world.

"It seems strange to me," Aidan continued. "Because the most universal language is love, isn't it? It's the thing we all understand. I look into your parents' heads, and it's all I see. All I see is love. All I see is love, for you."

CHAPTER 53

EMILY INHALED SHARPLY.

Aidan squeezed her hands, tighter. He was looking directly into her eyes, and she couldn't look away, and his eyes opened onto galaxies, onto spirals of stars and uncountable worlds.

"And you?" he said. "All I see in you is love too. For your parents. For Jeremy. For this beautiful world. Mountains! Snow! Sunlight! Trees! All of it is a miracle. But, Emily, you have to let it in."

"I don't understand," she said.

"My survival mechanism is to make myself something small. Something in need of protection. A little child."

She nodded. She managed to open her mouth. "I know."

"But yours, Emily," he said, "your survival mechanism, I think, is to remain as one."

"I don't—"

"—know what I mean? In your head right now, Emily, yes, you do." He gave her hands a final squeeze. "You act like you are trapped, powerless, like a child. Like your life is a prison. But what happens next is up to *you*."

"What happens next is that you leave me," she said.

"Oh, Emily," he said. "I will never leave you. We'll always be right here, together."

She felt herself frown. The weight of her eyebrows. "What?"

He squeezed her hands even tighter: that had always been his thing, squeezing her hands. "I'll show you," he said. "I'll show you what I showed Bob."

He squeezed her hands once more, and without warning or interval, she was in a state of darkness. Absolute darkness but with a sensation of space around her; deep space.

CHAPTER 54

NO: THERE WAS a pinprick of light, a glimmer, and it grew and grew and then it was the world she was seeing, the earth, from far away in space. But the land was all squashed together into a single mass, and the clouds seemed thin and strange, and gradually she realized: this was the earth millions and millions of years ago.

With a lurch, she flew forward, downward, closer in: until she could see the trees forming and falling and dying and the clouds and rain being made, and then life exploding, as the leaves sucked carbon from the atmosphere, making it possible for things built of cells to breathe. Bright lines of bacteria, becoming small strange creatures, and then under the sea with the coelacanths, and then up—into the air with the flying dinosaurs, and she saw the huge beasts below her, grazing and lifting their heads on long necks and bellowing into the clear, clear air—

and another lurch—

and suddenly there were mammals, more and more of them, bigger and bigger, and then apes that came down from trees and hunted and fished and spread around the world.

Grains grew up, cultivated. Forests fell.

Cities rose into the air and covered the earth.

People lived and died and lived and died, over and over, whole civilizations of people, and yet she saw the old die and babies born too, faster and faster and faster until she saw:

herself and her parents, sitting by a campfire—in the Adirondacks, she guessed, when she was small. Pine trees and wide spaces around them. They were holding sticks, speared through marshmallows, and they were roasting them over a blazing fire, and then eating them: sticky, stretchy, blackened: and laughing all the time, laughing together.

Emily had forgotten that. Had forgotten that it had been fun, sometimes.

Jump cut: herself, dancing alone in the studio in Minnesota, sweat shining on her skin.

Another jump cut: the jeers of the boys at the football game, that last one, their laughter, the bright lights of the stadium. Getting changed slowly, not wanting to be there but not wanting to go home, either; under a poster that said:

IF AT FIRST YOU DON'T SUCCEED, ADJUST YOUR PONYTAIL AND TRY AGAIN.

Emily was wearing a ponytail when she first saw that, and it almost made her want to take it out. The uniform was bad enough: a tight, long-sleeved top with a roaring bear on it; a short pleated skirt; pom-poms. How were pom-poms still happening in this day and age? Not to mention the skirt, which was just gross.

She was back in jeans and a sweatshirt when she left the changing room long after the other girls, and Brad was there, waiting in the corridor, just him and no one else around. Smoking a cigarette by a sign that said: NO SMOKING. Probably thought it made him look cool.

"You want one?" he said, holding it up. A challenge in the words; the gesture.

"Sure," she said.

A chink in his armor—his eyes registered surprise before he could get them under control. "OK," he said, reaching for his packet.

"I've got my own." She swung her bag around, took out her pack. She didn't smoke much. Just an occasional thing, a habit picked up from other ballet dancers. Those long hours waiting around in rehearsal, at exhibitions. But he didn't know that.

She took one out, lit it, and immediately regretted it. Now they had to stand there, smoking, until the cigarette was spent, when what she needed was to get out of there. She took a few drags and then crushed it under her heel. "Shoot," she said. "Forgot these were menthol. Gross."

He stepped forward, the confidence back in the set of his features. Leaned into her, as he'd done the other week, making his arms a cage. "You will go to prom with me," he said. "You just don't know it yet."

"Leave me alone."

"Not till you say yes."

And she ducked under his arm and twisted and spun—she was good at that, she was small and lithe and that was why she was the flyer on the team—and she was away from him, running down the hall and out the door, turning hard left and hiding behind the trees there, until her breathing slowed.

She texted Jeremy, told him what had happened, how nothing

had actually happened, but she had been scared. Trapped. Powerless.

Sounds like an a-hole, came the reply from her Minnesota friend.

A second message:

You should mess with his shit. Cut up his jersey or whatever those jocks wear.

She didn't really think about what happened next. Just found herself lingering until she saw Brad drive off, until she was able to slip back into the building and she was alone in the boys' locker room. She found his locker quickly: *Mecklenburg, B.* She tried the door.

Unlocked.

His varsity jacket or whatever it was called—she didn't know the names any more than Jeremy did—was hanging there. Various patches on it, and the school insignia. The mark of belonging, to the team.

Jackpot.

She took the jacket out and made a little pile of it in the middle of the floor and lit a cigarette. Her intention—as much as she was aware of it—was to burn the thing, to put some holes in it. She even made sure there was a sprinkler above her. It was meant to be a gesture, symbolic. Thinking of how he'd looked at her when he offered her the cigarette.

But the jacket was some kind of shiny material, and, as it turned out, incredibly flammable: it whooshed into flame, and she stepped back, alarmed, knocked into a chair, which fell over. The sprinkler didn't do anything. Maybe it wasn't switched on?

She ran out the door—she was sure she'd seen a fire extinguisher in the corridor—but when she returned to the locker room, the fire was already licking up the bottom of the door. How was that even possible? How had it spread so quickly? She backed away.

She backed away until she was outside, in the cool air, smoke already issuing from the windows of the building.

And that was where Miss Brady found her; she'd been doing final checks or something in the stadium, and when the alarm went off, she came running and found Emily there, still holding the cigarettes, the lighter.

"What's going on?" she'd shouted.

"I'm so sorry," said Emily. "It was an accident. I didn't . . . I didn't mean . . ."

Flames now were roaring up the walls of the building.

"You did this?" said Miss Brady.

Emily nodded.

"But . . . why?"

Emily didn't have the energy to explain—about moving to this goddamn place that was practically in the Arctic Circle, away from her best friend; about how cheerleading wasn't dance; about the awful uniform, the short skirt; the hot feeling of all those eyes in the crowd, on her body; about Brad's hand on her ass—the way he'd held her prisoner within his arms, the way they'd been alone, the way she'd wanted to get him back for that, to show him that he couldn't just do what he wanted.

So the locker room burned as they watched, as the firefighters arrived and trained their hoses on it, until the fire dampened, and smoked, and hissed.

Emily had thought the whole building might go up, but in the end it was just that one big room, the locker room, its ceiling and roof and walls burned so that the twisted, melted lockers were exposed to the sky, a blackened space missing from the structure, like a tooth from a mouth.

The boys' locker room, up in smoke. It did feel symbolic, though a step further than she'd wanted.

But as far as Miss Brady was concerned, it *was* what she'd wanted, because of that one stupid moment when she asked if Emily had done it, and Emily nodded, saying, "Yes, but it was an accident" instead of any of the other things she could and should have said.

She just went along with it: arson, immediate indefinite suspension pending an investigation, a call to her mom, who, in fact, was waiting in the parking lot outside, to take her home.

And then she went home, and her mom blew up, and she stormed out of the back door, and that was when—after slamming the door—she heard another loud noise and went into the woods behind their house to investigate, and found Aidan there, with his ship.

A stupid, angry, impetuous act, and it had turned her whole life upside down.

The memory shimmered, vanished, like a bubble bursting.

Oh, yes. It was Aidan; it was Aidan showing her this.

She was in the darkness of space again, stars all around.

Then:

She and Aidan were by the lake, dancing in the snow, her holding him and moving with him as if he were weightless, as if he were made to fit into her arms.

The whole moment shining, as if seen through a snow globe,

studded with the sparkle of stars. Perfect. Real too, even though it was past, still so real, as she watched them, him and her together, the vapor of their breath, the sound of their laughter, something like bells in the cold, but then—

Gone again, as time whisked her up to the present, and here she was, still with Aidan, outside the radio station, and there time stopped, bouncing hopefully in front of a white bright empty expanse: an emptiness she could fill, she realized, with whatever she wanted, a blankness to be written on with whatever story she wanted to tell—

And then she was zooming out again and the earth was tiny, brightly lit by the sun, a little glowing speck in blackness, and she knew that from this far away those millions of years would seem like nothing; from far enough away they would seem like an instant.

She watched the earth as the planets wheeled around her; the sugar-dust stars. Floating, she felt a kind of touch inside her mind, a nudge, a steer, from an intelligence far deeper and greater than her own and . . . she understood.

She understood what she was being shown.

She understood that the only thing that didn't exist was the future: that everything that was now and had been would always be, if you stepped far enough back, if you looked from far enough away. Because *now* was always becoming *then,* so what was the difference, really?

Right now, she was floating above the earth, but at every subsequent point in her life she would remember it as the past, and would that make it less real, less a true experience, simply because it was no longer at the surf's edge of the tide of time?

So: that moment by the lake with Aidan, dancing, was no less valid or vivid than now, which anyway was constantly being replaced by:

now—

And:

now—

And:

now.

The universe was being built out of tiny slices of the present, that was what she understood, that was the first part of the gift that was given to her, and some of those slices had Aidan in them and always would, and if you floated far enough from the earth and your view was wide-angle enough, there would seem no difference between the short time he was there and the rest of the world's history, and so Aidan couldn't really leave.

And: and she could do it herself, if she wanted, just by closing her eyes.

She understood too, though, the second part of the gift.

The present was a machine for making the past, she realized, but the material that fed that machine, its fuel, was the future: was everything that was yet to happen.

The past was always there. Aidan would never be gone.

But the future: the future was not yet real, and that meant that it was unwritten, that Emily could make it whatever she wanted to.

It was just bright blankness that she could fill with whatever she chose.

And nothing—not even Aidan—would ever really be gone.

CHAPTER 55

EMILY BLINKED BACK into the brightness of the beam from the spaceship, her eyes wet with tears.

"Thank you," she said.

Aidan shook his head. "Thank *you*," he said. "For finding me. For saving me."

She blinked away tears. "You're going, and I don't even know who you are," she said.

"I'm Aidan."

"I mean, who you really are."

"I'm really Aidan. And . . . something else."

Emily took in his small boy's body, his small boy's face. "But I've never really seen you; I don't know where you come from or anything . . ."

"I'll show you," he said.

He held her hand again, and he showed her. He showed her who he was, and who his people were and who they had been, in the history of the world, and how they had helped before, and how they were trying to help now.

"Oh," she said. "Oh." It was the most sensible utterance she could manage.

He looked up, as if hearing something. "But now I have to go," he said.

And then Aidan let go of her hand, and stepped away from her, and into the beam of light—and then it was gone, and so was he.

Somewhere, far away, she heard one of the men, speaking into a radio, she guessed. "We lost him," he said. "We lost him."

Emily fell to the ground.

CHAPTER 56

WHEN THE LIGHT went away and the world came back, Emily saw:

Her parents: her dad still holding a gun and her mom still hunched, ready to fight or run, but heads tilted, confused.

Then her mom saw Emily, lying on the ground, and she ran over, just started running, instantly, and then she was by Emily's side, lifting her up.

Emily also saw:

The two masked men, blinking.

A helicopter, approaching fast, from the mountains.

Then she heard it: *chukachukachukachuka*.

"What . . . What am I . . . I mean . . . ," said her dad, looking at the rifle in his hands.

One of the men stepped forward. "The boy is gone," he said. Snow in his tone. Coldness.

"What boy?" said Emily's dad.

Silence.

The two men looked at each other. Something passed between them, some sharing of understanding.

The one who had spoken took another step toward Emily's dad, who was no longer pointing the gun in any kind of threatening way. "It seems there's some sort of mix-up. If you could hand back the weapon, sir."

"Um," he said. "Yes. Of course. Um. Who are you?"

"That's . . . er . . . ," said the man.

"What's going on?" asked Emily's mom, who had her arms tight around Emily. "What's happening? Emily? Honey?"

Emily wondered why her mom was focusing on her, then realized it was because she had fallen. "I don't know," she said. She lied.

"The radio field . . . ," said the other man, the injured one—Emily could tell from the liquid rattle in his voice, his vowels thickened by the blood in his broken nose. "It must have scrambled you up somehow. We came to tell you to leave, and you, sir . . . , kind of lost it. Took my gun." Emily could also tell that he was thinking on his feet, that he could see Emily's parents were truly out of it, truly unaware of what had just happened.

"Shi—er—*shoot,*" said her dad. Ever the church man. "Training must have kicked in. I was Special Forces."

"So you said," said the man, not without bitterness.

Emily's dad handed back the gun. The man kept it low. The tension was mostly gone—just a strange atmosphere of bemusement and not knowing what to do, from this moment on.

One of the men spoke into his radio quietly. Giving a situation update, Emily guessed.

The *thwack* of the rotor blades was louder now, and the helicopter a big black presence that descended from the sky and landed by the jeep. A man got out—a man in a dark gray suit, with gray hair that almost matched, receding from his hairline. A man who radiated power and authority.

He stood for a moment, reading the scene. The downdraft flattened his hair. Emily saw vivid intelligence behind his gray eyes, a sense of quickness, even though he was perfectly still. She had never seen such motion in an unmoving person before, so much contained energy.

A man who would know what to do.

He walked briskly over to them.

"Mr. and Mrs. Perez?" he said. "Emily?"

"Yes," said Emily's mom, for all of them.

"Apologies for the heavy-handedness. This is a very sensitive laboratory. Our guards can be . . . a little overzealous when they believe someone has trespassed."

Emily's mom peered at the men with their masks, helmets, and rifles. "A *little*?" she said.

"I thought this was a university facility now," said Emily's dad. "Not military anymore."

"Correct," said the man. Emily noticed he hadn't introduced himself. She felt that was probably deliberate. "But we do a lot of work for the military, still. A lot of very secret work. You understand."

"Well, I wouldn't—"

"Good," said the man in the suit.

He nodded to the two men, who went back to the jeep and got in. They started the engine but didn't drive away.

"There wasn't . . . I don't think I saw a sign, telling us that . . . we weren't . . . I mean, that it was . . . ," said Emily's mom.

". . . private?" said the man. "Oh, there's a sign. Maybe you missed it. It happens."

"Oh," said her mom. "Oh. Sorry." A pause. Then a frown. "How do you know our names?"

"We must have run your plates," the man said, pointing to the pickup truck.

Emily looked at him sharply, and he looked back, and, *Oh no,* she thought, and immediately looked away, down, so he couldn't hold her gaze.

"I don't think that's . . . ours," said Emily's mom.

The man nodded slowly.

Tick tick tick went his mind, behind his eyes.

"You borrowed it, didn't you?" he said. "I mean, you must have. You're all over the news. Emily was in the small plane that crashed. I'm guessing you found her, and wanted to get her to a hospital right away to be checked over, and you thought this was some kind of medical center."

Emily's mind was turning. It struck her that if this man was saying this stuff, he was going to have to back it up. Make it real. Make people agree with his version of events. Which meant he was powerful. Very powerful. Were they on the news? But they were going to be, because he'd said so; she just felt that this was true.

Would the man whose truck they'd stolen from his driveway agree that they had borrowed it? And whoever *this* truck belonged to? *Yes,* she thought. Because the man in the suit would make it so.

"I . . . ," said Emily's dad. "Maybe. Yeah. I don't know. Sorry. This is very . . . It's very unlike us. I don't know how to explain it. Stealing a truck?"

The man smiled. It didn't reach his eyes. "Do not be concerned. I'm sure the police will take a lenient view. You were caring for your daughter, after all. I will put in a word for you." Emily noticed that her parents didn't question who this man was to be *putting in words* with the police. That was how disoriented they were. "I'm afraid you *will* need to leave, however."

"Of course," Emily's mom said. "But how? I mean, we can't just . . . take this . . . vehicle. Which isn't ours."

"I see," said the man. "Yes. Yes. We can drive you to Anchorage in the jeep." He raised a hand to the men sitting inside it, and one of them opened his door and got out. "We'll arrange a plane from there."

"Thank you," said Emily's dad. His brow was furrowed, like there was something that just wasn't adding up but he couldn't see what it was.

Her parents walked to the jeep, almost in a trance. Emily started to follow them, but the man in the suit stepped up next to her in a way that she knew was meant to make her stop, and the annoying thing was, it did.

"I'm sorry for your ordeal," he said. "The plane crash. Everything."

"Thank you," she said.

A pause.

"A mercy your little brother was not injured, either." He said it so lightly, so quickly. Clever. She could see how it might work, on the right person.

She pulled her face into confusion. "I don't have a little brother," she said.

His face remained very still, watching hers. He blinked, once.

"Perhaps I misheard the news," he said eventually. He spoke slowly, but his eyes moved all the time. They were eyes that, she imagined, were always looking for something to analyze.

Like her.

"I guess," she said after a pause. "Can I go now?"

He held an arm out, showing the way. "I was never going to stop you."

She didn't say anything. She left him behind. Then she turned. No one could hear them from the jeep.

"You can make things happen, right?" she said.

He didn't say anything for the longest time; awareness crackled between them, electrifying the air; then he nodded slightly.

"Bob. The pilot. He's up at the lake, still. Or Mountain Rescue may have got to him. Anyway. Make sure he's OK."

"Yes," he said. No hesitation. "I will."

Another pause.

"I may come and speak to you, one day," he said. "If that's all right. About . . . the crash. About your experience. For . . . academic interest."

She thought about that. He was watching her. His eyes were not unkind. And there was a *force* behind them, that kinetic thing, spinning, whirring. She almost . . . admired it. She had never met anyone like this before. Not in her small town.

"Why?" she said. She let it creep into her voice: that she knew that he knew that she knew. It was so dizzying, the layers of it.

"I think you are very interesting," he said. "A very interesting person, indeed."

"OK," she said. "But why would I want to speak to you?"

She kept her eyes on him. If he said the wrong thing, it would be over, and he knew it, and knew that she knew that he knew it, and she saw the moving machine, all its parts so densely packed and spinning, all its cogs and gears, behind those gray eyes of his.

"We can make stolen pickup trucks go away," he said. "Think of what else we can—"

"That had better not be a threat," she said. "Think of what I can do too. Think of what I can *tell*."

"I was going to say: think of what else we can do to help you," he said. "You want to get out of your little town, right? I've seen your social media. We can help with that."

She kept her eyes trained on his. "Don't lie to me."

"I don't lie," he said.

His eyes didn't move. He was telling the truth. She knew it, somehow. And anyway it was nice that there was someone else who *knew what had really happened.* Who remembered. It kept Aidan there, in some kind of a way.

"I probably don't have much choice," she said. "I mean, you know where I live." She rolled her eyes, and he laughed, surprised.

She got in the jeep and shut the door.

"What did he want to talk about?" said her mom from the other side of the back bench.

"Oh, nothing," said Emily.

It was the worst: the worst teenage lie ever, and any mom in her right mind would have called her on it. But her mom was not in her right mind.

The jeep pulled away.

Emily closed her eyes, and traveled in time. They were in

the little plane, waiting to take off, and Aidan was beside her. He smiled. Squeezed her hand the way he always did; she even felt it.

She opened her eyes, and he was gone, the future in front of her, untraveled, a road waiting to be driven down.

They drove.

CHAPTER 57

EMILY PICKED UP her homework from her locker and headed out of school. It was a low building, concrete, built for maximum heat insulation in winter.

"See you at the game?" called Kelly, her hand on her car door.

Emily smiled. "Yeah," she said.

And it was true: she'd be there, supporting—but absolutely not cheerleading. Her suspension was over, and to her surprise, coming back had not been too awful. She'd expected to be ostracized, to be whispered about. Well, there was a bit of that, but it was more excited whispering than cruelty: she was the girl who had survived a plane crash, after all, and then walked down off a mountain. She was pretty sure that was one reason she'd been allowed back—she was famous now, at least briefly, and the school wanted to look forgiving because of the trauma she'd experienced.

One reason.

What went unsaid: that everyone assumed she'd stowed away

on the plane in order to escape the humiliation, in order to flee from the little town where she was the arson girl.

She was *still* the arson girl, of course, the girl who had burned down part of the school; she knew it would take some time to get past that, but even then—it was high school, wasn't it? There was hardly a kid there who hadn't dreamed of burning the place down. She was just the one who'd actually done it. Or rather, who had smoked a cigarette in secret, in the boys' locker room, and then carelessly discarded the butt—that was her story, and she was sticking to it.

And Miss Brady was going along with it. From the way the teacher looked at her, Emily had a feeling she had a lot of questions: about the cigarette, about what she had been doing in the locker room in the first place. But she didn't ask them. Emily suspected the man with the gray eyes had something to do with that—that he had exerted pressure of some kind, influence.

"We'll keep it off your school record," Miss Brady had said. "We don't want to throw away your future because of one mistake."

No. No, Emily did not want to throw away her future. Not anymore.

And later, in return, she'd filmed a special with Miss Brady for the local news crew: the head teacher shaking her hand, welcoming her warmly back to school.

As if nothing had ever happened.

So: she'd been hanging out with Kelly, with Madison, with Eric, with Tyrese. It was—and again, she was surprised—kind of fun. It was as if something had changed inside her, since Aidan.

None of them remembered Aidan, of course.

She climbed into her old blue Ford F-150–eighty thousand miles on the clock, but her dad had checked it over and reconditioned the engine before he and her mom gave it to her.

"Thought you could use a little more independence," her mom had said.

"And if you lose the keys, you know how to get in," said her dad.

There was an awkward silence, and then they laughed. They tried not to talk too much about the time after the plane crash— her parents told themselves a story about it, that they'd been in a rush to get to civilization, but Emily could tell they only partly believed it, and that the best way for them to reconcile the events with the kind of people they understood themselves to be was to not think about it.

Emily started the engine and turned up the heat. It was nearly summer but still cold when the sun was going down, as it was now.

There was a knock on the truck window. Emily turned, startled.

Brad winked at her from the other side of the glass. She wound it down. Manually—it took forever, cranking the little handle.

He winked at her again. "Hey, beautiful," he said.

She didn't say anything.

"So . . . ," he said. "I still don't have a date for prom. Been kinda . . . reserving the spot for you."

Emily laughed, despite herself, at his unflinching self-confidence, his ironclad self-belief.

"No, thanks," she said.

His eyes hardened. "I'll just have to ask again tomorrow."

She took a breath. "Brad," she said. His small stony eyes. "You know who I am, right? I'm the girl who burned down the locker room because a football player made me mad. I walked away from a plane that crashed and exploded. I did things you would not *believe,* things the papers have not reported. I came down off a mountain with a man who had sepsis, and lived. A bear attacked us, and we walked away."

He bit his lip.

"So, Brad, dude. Listen. If you 'ask me on a date' again, if you approach me again—hell, if you approach *any* of the girls at this school again—I am going to come for you, OK? And it will be when you least expect it."

She gunned the engine, made the tires squeal, and left him standing there, mouth open, as if the Alaskan air might blow right through his head, where his brains should be.

CHAPTER 58

SHE DROVE PAST the town's small strip of stores: hardware, hunting and fishing supplies, groceries. As the houses ran out, she pulled up to the airstrip. She'd heard he was here: that was what some of the whispering at school had been about.

She drove in and parked in a bay that said: PICK UP AND DROP OFF ONLY in peeling white paint.

A sleepy-looking guy was on the security desk. He waved her through, and the barrier lifted. She walked across what was laughably referred to as the terminal—a single kiosk, currently closed, where you could buy chewing gum and water—and then outside. There was a mechanic standing around. She asked for directions, and he told her, pointed the way.

She zipped up her jacket and walked briskly past the single hangar to the plane sitting on the short runway. Beyond, the setting sun lit the hills.

It was another bush plane. The De Havilland was destroyed, of course, and now he was flying a beautifully restored Super Cub painted in blue and yellow. It had fat tires mounted, so he wasn't going on a lake run but on a trip to some other airfield elsewhere in the enormous state.

He had a panel open; was inspecting some element of the engine.

"Hey," she said.

Bob turned, and smiled. "Hey, yourself," he said. "If you're planning to stow away, I'm leaving at six a.m. sharp tomorrow."

"Ha-ha," she said. "Just . . . wanted to say hello. Properly, you know, without my parents there. And the press, and whatever."

The media had turned up for her reunion with Bob, when he was helicoptered back to town: the girl and the pilot who had survived the mountains, until he had become too sick to continue, until he had nobly urged her on.

(She had made Bob the hero in the story. It was the least he deserved.)

The local newspaper had been there, obviously, but also TV—several channels—and someone from BuzzFeed. They'd done a story on it, complete with photos of bears, and avalanches, and lean-to shelters.

(But no guns.)

But it had meant not talking about Aidan. And Aidan was what she wanted to talk about.

"I was wondering . . . ," she said.

He put the wrench he was holding into a steel toolbox, and looked around before meeting her eyes. ". . . if I remember him," he said.

"Yeah." Relief in her voice, like moonlight in ice. Making it glow.

He did. He remembered.

He nodded, even though he'd already answered the question. "Of course I do. Your parents?"

"No."

"That must be weird. I mean, understatement of the century."

"It's . . . Yeah," she said.

"Yeah."

"Did you speak to your wife?" she said.

"Yep," he said. "And we're still speaking."

She thought about what Aidan had shown her: how everything that had happened was still there, how nothing was ever lost. She thought about what that might mean, a vision like that, to someone who had lost a son.

"What Aidan showed you. Did it have to do with time?" she asked. "Like . . . the present and the past, and how they're always there?"

"Yeah. He showed you too?"

"Yeah. Did you tell your wife?"

"Did I tell my wife that an alien touched me and I saw that our son will never really die? No."

She nodded. That made sense.

"Explaining it . . . It's not quite the same as him showing you— you know?" he said. "Still. It helped. Me and Melanie, we're going out to dinner next month. Baby steps. But better than not moving at all."

"Good," said Emily. "That's good. I'm glad." She *was* glad: she felt a pang in her heart at the thought of Bob and his wife meeting up again, with their lost son always between them. Though, with what Aidan had shown them—perhaps not so lost as all that. Perhaps as present and as real as anything that had ever happened or was happening or ever would happen.

That was the gift Aidan had given, to her, and to Bob, and to Bob's wife, Melanie. The past was always there. The future was waiting to be shaped.

But, of course, it had been a trial too: the crash and everything after; it had been violent and scary and draining. She took a step back and examined Bob. She noticed, not without a twinge of guilt, that there were new lines on his face; creases around his eyes and a certain hollowness to his cheeks. His left arm was hanging a little oddly.

"How's the wound?" she said.

"Healed now," he said. "But it aches in the cold."

"Sorry."

"Don't be: it's a good luck charm at every airstrip and airport in the state. I crashed and lived to tell the tale. I may never pay for whiskey again. And whiskey helps with the pain."

She laughed.

He looked up, at the mountains and the sky above them. So did she.

"You think . . . you think he's still there? You think he can see us?" she said.

There was silence for a while.

"The other day, I was flying west of Juneau," he said. "Saw a shimmer in the sky beside me, out the port window. Like there was something shiny, just out of sight."

Like fish scales behind the air, thought Emily. "Oh," she said. "Do you think . . . do you think he . . ."

She didn't need to complete her question.

Bob lifted his bad arm, and put his hand on her shoulder. "Kid, I think he can always see you. I think he'll watch over you. That's what I think."

She smiled a little. "Really?" It was a nice thought: that Aidan might miss her too. That he might care.

"Really. I mean, he can't come back, right? At least not now. The place is crawling with feds."

This was true. Men and women in face masks and bio suits had been all over the woods behind Emily's house. They'd told her parents they were with the EPA. They hadn't found anything, though, or at least Emily didn't think so. They'd have needed heavy equipment, and she didn't see anything like that. At some point, Aidan and his people must have removed the ship.

The man with the gray eyes hadn't been to talk to her yet: but she knew he would. One day.

"And . . . ," continued Bob. "His thing is to make himself small, so that you protect him, right? But I figure . . . I figure he protected us too. So why would he stop?"

"Huh," she said.

Yeah.

Why would he stop?

"What did he say, anyway?" said Bob. "When he . . . left. Did he say goodbye?"

She thought for a moment. "No," she said. "No, he didn't."

Bob smiled. "Well, there you go."

CHAPTER 59

THE SECOND TIME Emily saw the man with the gray eyes, he was in the coffee shop, and she knew he was there to see her.

When she went inside—immediately taking off her jacket because Mrs. Cartwright always kept the place hot—he was sitting alone at a table near the back.

She walked over. His restless, analytical eyes followed her all the way.

"Ms. Perez," he said.

"Mr...."

"Smith will do."

"But it's not your name."

"No."

She shrugged, and sat down.

"You want coffee?" he asked.

"I'll take mint tea." She didn't like mint tea, or at least she didn't know if she liked it, but she wanted to sound like someone who knew what to order, right away—someone decisive. Powerful.

He waved over Martina, whom Emily knew from cheerleading

and who was in her senior year, and ordered. Martina took one short look at Emily, which might have been because of the fire and the getting suspended, or it might just have been because she was wondering why Emily was in the coffee shop with a much older man.

Either way: Emily didn't care.

"So, we took care of the stolen trucks. The pilot. Everything." Mr. Smith was watching her as he said this.

She just looked at him blankly. To thank him, to acknowledge what he was saying, would be to admit that she was not like her parents: to submit to a version of events where she had understood what was happening, where she knew what Aidan was.

Which, of course, they both knew was the case. But she was being contrary. She wanted to resist, as long as possible.

"How's school?" he asked.

She kept her face neutral. "Was that you too?" she said. "The school letting me come back? The police dropping the charges?"

He shrugged.

"Shall I take that as a yes?"

He shrugged again.

"If you're just going to shrug like that, why did you want to talk to me?"

"Your parents don't remember what really happened," he said. "Don't remember *him*. Which is usual." His eyes seemed to focus in closer on her; like the twist of a lens on a camera. "But you and Mr. Simpson do. Which is unusual." He paused. "*Unusual* is perhaps the wrong word. This is hardly a common occurrence. So let us say *unprecedented*."

"I don't know what you're talking about," she said.

"Yes, you do."

Emily took a sip of her mint tea. It was weird. Like drinking candy, except not as sweet as candy. She didn't say anything.

"If you're not going to talk about him, why did you come in and sit with me?" the man asked.

She sighed. "I just . . . I don't know."

"You're pleased—part of you is pleased—to speak to someone else who knows. Someone other than the pilot. I mean, your parents being oblivious. It must be difficult."

He was completely right, of course, and she realized in that moment that was why she had come in. Because this man, Mr. Smith, whatever his real name was, knew who Aidan was. Remembered Aidan.

"Maybe," she said. "Something like that."

His eyes stilled for a moment, brightened. He was rolling a pen along his fingers, but he didn't seem to have any paper or notepad of any kind to write on. "Have you seen him again? Since?"

"Aidan?"

"If that's what you want to call him."

She shook her head. "Of course not."

"OK. If you do, call me." He pushed a card over to her. It had a phone number on it, nothing else. "What about . . . anything he left with you. A gift? Bob said he gave him a gift, that he might have given one to you as well. It is important you tell us anything he gave or . . . communicated . . . to you."

She noticed him omitting Bob's surname: an attempt to establish intimacy.

"Bob said that?"

"Hmm."

"Did he tell you what the gift was?" She hoped the answer was . . .

"No."

Good, she thought.

"Well," she said, out loud. "Can't you torture it out of him? Isn't that what you guys do?"

"This is America," said Mr. Smith. "Not Russia."

"Are you sure?" she said.

"Touché," he said. "But don't quote me on that."

"Also," she said, "your men shot at me. A lot. You'll forgive me if that kind of sticks in my throat. It's not an easy thing to forgive, someone trying to kill you."

He sat back in his chair. "Wait—you think we were trying to kill you?"

She blinked at him. "Yes. Obviously."

He spread his hands, a gesture of: *The things I have to deal with.* "Our men all had orders to keep you alive," he said. "Warning shots only. This isn't a movie."

"They shot Bob when all he'd done was wave at them."

Mr. Smith shook his head. "I wasn't there. But I imagine they thought he was armed."

She made a face of: *Yeah, good one, tell me another.*

"Emily," he said. Long-suffering tone—*I'm being rational here, and you're being hysterical.* "We're not in the business of shooting teenage girls."

"So Bob was acceptable collateral?"

Silence.

"Is that a yes?"

He sighed. "We're not in the business of shooting teenage girls," he said again. "Nor are we in the business of torturing those who have had . . . encounters. And the pilot wasn't talking. So, please: tell me about the gift. What did Aidan give you?"

"Why do you want to know?" she said.

He looked at her with frank stupefaction. "Security," he said. "My job is to protect the integrity of the United States."

"What he gave me . . . It has nothing to do with that."

"We'll make that judgment, I think," he said. "What was it—an object? A map?"

"No."

"Something he told you or showed you, then?"

"Yes," she said.

"What? A weapon? Instructions? Clean power? Renewable energy?"

"Are you serious?" she said.

"Are you *not*?" he retorted. "This is vital military intelligence. I don't know why you can't grasp the import of all this."

"Military?"

He sighed again. "This . . . creature . . . violated U.S. airspace. Landed. Evaded capture. Then went away again, after showing God knows what to a pilot and a girl. We have to protect our territory."

She thought of when she sat with Aidan outside the cabin, him talking about how men always wanted to own bits of the world, how to them, this marvelous, this miraculous land was often only *territory*. She thought how absurd that must have seemed from his wide-angle view of the world.

She realized she was smiling only when she saw Mr. Smith frowning.

"I fail to see the humor in all this," he said.

"No," she said. "It's not funny. It's just . . ."

"Yes?"

"You wouldn't understand what he showed me. You *can't* understand. Your whole . . . your whole way of looking at the world. How you believe everything is yours to question, analyze, dissect. The way you think everything is war. You will never understand what he knows, or what he is."

"Do *you* know what he is? Where he comes from?"

"Yes," she said. She thought of the last thing Aidan had shown her, and smiled again at the thought of explaining such knowledge to this man.

"Then tell me."

"I can't. I would have to show you, and I can't do that, either."

Mr. Smith leaned back, fingers steepled. "Then tell me what he showed you. Tell me his gift. We can help you, you know. We have funds. We can ensure you a brighter future."

She stood. This was a pointless conversation. She'd wanted to talk to someone who would understand, and she knew now that this man would never understand; his own intelligence, his inductive mind, prevented it. She thought briefly about what she was throwing away—what he'd said about helping, giving her a brighter future, how he'd implied they could support her in wanting to dance.

Well. Screw it.

She was going to have to sort that out herself, with her parents—make them understand, somehow, that she needed dance in her life. Maybe she could go back to Minnesota sometimes, train with Jeremy and his mom. Maybe Bob would give her a discount on flights.

"But that's just it," she said. "There is no future, bright or otherwise. Not yet anyway. The future is whatever I make of it."

She started to leave.

"What?" he said. "What's that supposed to mean?"

"Well," she said, turning. "I did say you wouldn't understand."

And then she walked out.

CHAPTER 60

WHEN EMILY CAME downstairs the next morning, her parents were both in the kitchen. She could smell that her mom was cooking something delicious, and it wasn't even Sunday—it was a school day. Usually, her dad would have left early, to prepare for his lessons. At the breakfast bar, her plate was laid out, her cutlery, her glass.

And next to them, a laptop, open.

Her mom's laptop.

Which her mom was standing next to, half smiling, half embarrassed.

"Um...," said Emily. "What's this?"

Her dad nodded to her mom. Her mom woke the screen by tapping the touchpad, and YouTube popped up. She pressed play on a view of mountains, it looked like.

Emily took a step closer.

She saw: 7,789,005 views.

She saw: "Girl dances in the snow."

There was no sound: and then there was. Gentle violins,

tracing a delicate melody. The footage was wobbly, woozy, almost as if filmed through water, and then she realized: no. Not water. A plastic window, in a cabin.

Outside the window, she, Emily, swam into focus. Snow was falling around her as slowly she began to dance. She almost glided across the stones of the narrow beach, white mountains behind her, the lake shimmering in the moonlight. The snow fell as she spun and leaped into the air, and the music swelled, accompanying her; she seemed to hang suspended, like the snowflakes, as if gravity had exempted her temporarily, and her feet and hands drew long shapes in the air as she pirouetted and stretched and crouched and arched her back, her body speaking in a language of movement and form.

"Oh," she said.

The dance continued: it was mesmerizing, even she could see that, with the stars and the snow. She saw something else: she was good—it was something she was good at; it was something her body fit into, the movement of the dance, like worn old clothes.

Bob must have been filming from inside the cabin. Next time she saw him she was going to kill him.

Then: she caught her breath. In the video, she reached out her hands, pulled an invisible partner into a turn, her arms encircling empty space: Aidan. Except he wasn't there; she couldn't see him; the viewers of the video couldn't see him.

As if he'd never been there.

As if he'd never existed.

She danced, with an invisible partner, and then, just as the video neared its end, her feet left the ground and didn't return to it; she floated up, into the night air, above the lake, and slowly rotated there, as if held up by ropes, but there were no ropes, and then—

The video ended.

Emily's mom scrolled down, to the comments.

Emily saw: *this girl was born to dance.*

She saw: *who is this?! someone needs to find her.*

She saw: *amazing. such talent.*

She saw: *HOW DID THEY DO THAT BIT AT THE END?!*

Her mom closed the laptop.

"I didn't know he was filming that, I swear—"

"It's OK," said her dad, holding up a hand. "Your mom and me, we just want to talk to you . . . about . . . this."

"We never really addressed . . . what happened at school," said her mom. "The arson. I'm not sure why."

I know why, thought Emily. Because that was when Aidan turned up.

She didn't say that, though.

She noticed too that they didn't mention the part at the end of the video, the part where she seemed to fly. Averting their eyes from the sun of full awareness.

"Listen . . . ," she said. "About that. I never meant to burn anything down. And I wasn't smoking, like I told Miss Brady. It was . . . There was a guy who kind of . . . Well, he was pushy. Wouldn't take no for an answer. I wanted to burn a hole in his football jacket, or whatever. Teach him a lesson. That was all."

Her parents exchanged a look. "We wondered," said her dad.

"Really?"

Her mom did a strange smile. "Well. Not specifically. But we felt like . . . something was off. We're your parents. We like to think we know you pretty well."

"You need any help?" said her dad. "With this guy?"

"I think I've got it covered," said Emily. "But I'll let you know."

He nodded.

"We're not . . . cruel, you know," said her mom. "You hated cheerleading, right? I don't think I understood that, not quickly enough, anyway."

"Yeah," said Emily.

"But you love to dance?" her mom continued. "I mean, you can just see it on that video."

Emily nodded.

"I'm sorry," said her mom. "For pushing you, for pushing you with the cheerleading stuff. I think I just . . . I didn't get it. The dancing, and what it meant to you. I mean, you never said how much you wanted to do it. I just thought it was . . ."

"Pointless?" said Emily.

Her mom swallowed. "I don't know. Maybe. I didn't get it. But you love it, right? It's something that's important to you."

"Yes."

"Something you'd fight for."

Emily and her mom were looking into each other's eyes. "Yeah," Emily said.

"Because you're a fighter. Like us."

Emily looked at her mom's motivational magnets. YOU DON'T KNOW YOUR OWN STRENGTH. "Yes," she surprised herself by saying.

Her dad leaned over and gave her an awkward hug. Her mom kissed the top of her head.

284

"OK," they said together.

Then her dad picked up a brochure from the sideboard, handed it to her.

She looked at it. On the front was a picture of a row of young men and women, their hands on a barre, the background blurring into indistinctness, the foreground crisp and light and glowing.

Summer Dance Intensive at the Juilliard School, said the type underneath.

She held it in her hands. She looked up at her parents.

"It's three weeks," said her dad. "In the summer. We thought . . . if it went well, if you liked it . . . then it could be like a stepping-stone."

"A stepping-stone?"

"To college."

She opened it. Saw the course fees. Looked up again. "This is expensive," she said.

"They offer scholarships," said her mom. "For gifted students. Tuition only, but your dad and I can cover the accommodations."

"Oh," said Emily. "I'm sure they won't—"

"You think eight million people who saw that video are wrong?" said her mom. "We're responsible parents; we keep track of the comments. At first we wanted to tell Bob to take it down, but then . . . One of the people who commented is a professor at Juilliard. She wanted to know who the girl in the video was."

"You'd have to apply, of course," said her dad. "Record a video of your dancing. I guess that's taken care of. Ha-ha. Personal statement too. But you have two months. If you work hard, train every day, I'm sure you'll get it."

Her dad: ever the military mindset. Discipline. Training.

"You can do anything, if you put your mind to it," said her mom.

Her mom: motivational queen.

"The future doesn't exist yet," said Emily. "I can make it what I want."

"Um . . . yeah," said her dad.

She scanned the brochure. Three weeks. Classical and modern dance. On-campus accommodations. Forty-four students from all around the country.

There was no way she'd get in—but it was worth a shot, wasn't it? She'd survived a mountain, an avalanche, men with guns. She could fill out an application.

"Thank you," she said. "Really. Thank you."

She got up and hugged her mom—and her dad hugged her too, so she was in between—a hug sandwich, they'd called it when she was little; she was the cheese, and they were the slices of bread.

"Love you, kid," said her dad.

Her mom tousled her hair.

"Love you too," Emily said.

"There are blueberry pancakes," said her dad. "You eat them quickly, you could do a half hour's dance practice before school."

Emily smiled. Her mom carried over a stack of pancakes, drenched in blueberry syrup.

They were good.

They were pretty incredible, in fact.

There was something gnawing at Emily, though, some sharp-toothed thing inside, and she wasn't sure what it was.

Something to do with what her mom had said: about how they hadn't talked about the arson, at the time . . .

And . . .

That was it.

They hadn't talked about it, because Aidan had come. He had come just when she needed him.

Was that a coincidence? she wondered for the first time. Maybe it wasn't. Maybe it wasn't a coincidence that he'd appeared, with his ship, just when she'd been thrown out of school, just when she was at her most vulnerable.

Wasn't that what he did?

Hadn't he said he couldn't help it?

Perhaps it was part of his protective mechanism: he made himself something small, something in need of protection, but maybe it was more than that too. Perhaps he homed in on people's distress signals, or their loneliness; perhaps he could somehow feel who it was who would take him in and make him their own.

There were other houses next to theirs, after all, other houses backing onto the woods. Other people who could have been made to hear the sound of the ship.

Had he ever felt what she felt?

Had he ever been hers, her little Aidan, or was it all an act?

She thought of the video: how he wasn't there, how her arms had closed on the thinnest mountain air. She thought of how he'd erased the memory of the fire from her parents' minds, how he'd promised not to do it to her.

But what if that was what he'd been doing all along? Making a story, in her mind, so that he could use her.

"What's wrong, honey?" asked her mom.

Emily brushed her cheek. A tear was tracking down it. "Nothing," she said.

That was true on one level: it was nothingness that was wrong; the nothingness where Aidan had been.

Then something made Emily look up.

Outside the window, the leaves were growing larger and greener every day, the trees seeming to expand. A bird flew past, landed on a branch. A camp robber, just like the one at the cabin where they'd stayed, by the lake, with Aidan.

But it wasn't the flight of the camp robber that had caught her eye, it was something else, it was . . .

The bird chittered, singing to the lightening sky.

No: not just lightening, Emily realized, not just lit by the sun that was rising.

Shining.

The sky was shining.

CHAPTER 61

EMILY HAD ONLY eaten two of her three pancakes, but she slid back her chair. "I'm just going outside," she said.

"Why?" said her mom.

"I guess I got used to it," she said slowly, thinking on her feet. How could she explain that there was a strange light, and she thought it might be an alien ship? "Being outside, I mean," she continued. "On the mountain. The air. The birds. The sunlight. You know?"

Her dad grinned, pleased. "Yeah, I know."

"So I just wanna be out in it for a moment," Emily said. "In the light." This was an evasion that had the benefit of being literally true.

"OK, honey, but don't be long," said her mom. "School starts in an hour."

Emily glanced at the shimmering sky. "I'll be back in a minute," she said.

"Sure," said her mom. "Put on a coat—it's still cold out there."

Emily did: she put on a coat, and she went out of the back

door, and through the trees. As she walked, she took out her phone and typed a message for Jeremy. He was real, he was human, and she hadn't talked to him in ages. He'd sent her messages, of course—she'd been on TV; trending on Twitter. But she hadn't texted back until now. She hit *Send*.

Summer intensive at Juilliard. applying. you in?

A pause, then a ping. And Jeremy—amazing Jeremy—didn't even mention all the texts she hadn't returned.

Sure. anything for you. saw you on the news, BTW. WHAT HAS BEEN GOING ON, GIRL? your life is crazy.

She texted back:

You have literally no idea.

Another ping:

Can't wait. Xxx.

She smiled and put away the phone. Then she carried on, to where she had first seen Aidan, where his ship had crashed. Twigs snapped, and leaves from the previous autumn crunched underfoot, laced with morning frost.

When she arrived, though, at the small clearing, there was nothing there.

Just a bare space, an indentation where the trees had been flattened, a kind of furrow, already filling with vegetation. To the side, some of the trees that had been broken were now divided into neat piles of sectioned trunk, waiting to be turned by her dad into logs for burning. Other than that, nothing . . .

But no.

Because then she saw it: a small object in the very middle of the circular, concave clearing.

She went to it, and stooped, and picked it up. She turned it over in her hands, marveling at it. The material was like nothing she had ever seen before: nothing that existed on Earth, she was sure, straightaway. It was smooth and hard and yet warm to the touch: like a cross between wood and stone but with the dull gleam of metal.

It was a figurine.

It was a little boy. A little boy, formed perfectly from this strange substance, a little boy with messy hair and a smile on his face.

It was Aidan.

She thought of the carved wooden girl she had given him in the woods, the one she had spent all night whittling. This was infinitely finer, and she knew she could never show it to anyone, especially not the man with the gray eyes who wanted to ask her questions. She also knew she would keep it with her, forever, until the last day of her life.

She held it close for a moment, then put it into the fur-lined pocket of her jacket.

She looked up: a cloud hung overhead, cumulonimbus, backlit even though the low sun was behind her: backlit impossibly, a sort of fish-scale shimmer that existed somewhere at the edge of vision, not the edge as in the corners, but the edge as in almost invisible, as in only faintly visible.

She put up both her hands, and crossed them above her head, a universal gesture, she hoped, a greeting, a way to say hello. Then she opened them, and crossed them again, and again, waving. The wave of a person wanting to be rescued, though she didn't need to be rescued anymore. She did it with big movements, with all the strength she could muster. Clasped her hands over her heart.

A way to say I love you.

For a second, the brightness increased—someone turning up the dimmer switch on the whole sky—and the cloud above seemed to burn, to glow like a fresco from long ago on some Italian ceiling, all the smoke-ribboned light of heaven, shooting beams through the clouds; all the incomprehensible majesty.

She remembered Aidan, speaking outside the cabin.

It's beautiful, he had said.

Yes.

Then, just as quickly, the light disappeared, and there was only a gunmetal sky, and a cloud moving slowly across it. He was gone. But she thought of one of her mom's motivational magnets, which had never made sense to her before: EVERYTHING YOU NEED IS INSIDE YOU.

It made sense now.

She lowered her arms.

She smiled to herself, and turned, and walked back toward the house.

Into the future.